ONE

'MIGHTY MAGIC.'

Around midnight, with a soft-moaning wind stirring eerily in the trees around that fire-reddened glade, they began the Ordeal By Flames.

But now the victim, tied to the stake outside the lodge of the tribal medicine man, was exhausted and near to the end of his strength. He had suffered the torments and tortures of his Kittewa brothers for many hours, and, besides, he felt weak from his three days of solitary fasting within sound of his enemy's camp.

Now he felt that he could not hold up his head any longer. He was sure he would flinch and show fear when the bone-rattling hideously masked medicine man came running at him with his blazing torches.

Yet he knew that he could not show fear – dare not – for if he did he would be beaten out of the tribe, never to return. The shame of it, to be an outcast from his tribe, would be more than he could stand,

5

he realised, and he steeled himself anew to last out these final few minutes.

His weary, pain-glazed eyes flickered to the deep shadows beyond the circle of lodges. His eyes were looking for someone – a maiden who would be his when finally he came through this initiation ceremony.

He thought he saw her, a slim, shy creature in soft doeskin. Lovely Gentle Fawn, so well named.

Thinking of her brought strength, so that his head lifted proudly, and he flashed fierce, challenging young eyes towards the big fire where the medicine man was chanting medicine talk over two torches which had been brought to him.

He would survive, he vowed. This was to be the last of his ordeals. If he showed courage now, as he had done during all the previous tests, within the hour he would have been admitted to his warrior society and would be a fighting man in the tribe and a youth no longer.

His raw nerves jumped at a sudden scream from the medicine man, who had lighted his torches and was now dancing around the fire. The warriors of the tribe, seated in a wide circle around the staked young Indian, watched impassively as the medicine man began to dance his way towards his victim.

Just within the forest a Kittewa dog soldier, on sentry for his tribe, caught the scrape of dry branch upon dry branch as the sighing wind stole through the trees. It was like the ghostly passage of some chill presence, and the sentry's eyes widened and rolled with superstitious fear.

N

Railroad Saboteurs

To the Kittewas, Careless O'Connor was the feared enemy, a man of great power and possessor of magical gifts. The thieving, murdering tribesmen were warned not to hinder the construction of a railroad and O'Connor was there to frighten them into living in peaceful co-existence with the white man.

But there was a limit to what even he could achieve and soon there was open warfare.

Careless would need to use his every skill if he were to keep the warlike Kittewas at bay and worse still, find and bring to justice the renegade white men who were sabotaging the railroad.

Railroad Saboteurs

Gordon Landsborough

A Black Horse Western

ROBERT HALE · LONDON

ISBN 0 7090 7314 3

Robert Hale Limited
Clerkenwell House
Clerkenwell Green
London EC1R 0HT

Typeset by
Derek Doyle & Associates, Liverpool.
Printed and bound in Great Britain by
Antony Rowe Limited, Wiltshire

Something moved. That was all. A shadow darker than the darkest shadows was in one place one moment and in another a fraction of a second later.

The sentry looked unhappily back to where the ceremonial fire glowed warm and bright. There were his friends, companions. Here, alone on the edge of the stirring, shadowy forest, was fear – and danger.

That sentry could not see anything threatening, yet in his bones he felt there was an enemy at hand.

Reluctantly his eyes came dragging away from the initiation ceremony over by the fire. They sought deep into the bushes around him, yet they saw nothing.

There was nothing to see. In that moment that he looked towards the fire, that darker shadow had glided past him. Now the enemy most feared by the Kittewas had passed through the circle of guarding sentries.

The ordeal was almost over. The medicine man had made his play before the face of his helpless victim, flashing the flaming torches so close that the heat scorched and his eyebrows and lashes singed off into burnt little curls and his eyeballs hurt from the intensity of the glow.

Yet they never closed; he never flinched. A chorus of grunted approval arose from the warriors. Truly this youth was worthy to become a warrior of the tribe. He had borne his tests like a man. He was a man, they chorused, rising to their feet.

The medicine man seemed reluctant to end the ceremony, however. He was an evil-smelling man, held in awe because of the power of his medicine. He liked to torment youths during these ceremonies – liked even more to torture captive warriors from some other tribe.

But he recognised that in the eye of the elders of the tribe the youth had survived this ordeal, and he was wise enough not to prolong the proceedings whatever his private wishes.

So he made the medicine talk that would finally make the youth the warrior he wanted to be. He gave him his name by which he would be known among the tribe, and then he went forward to whisper in the boy's ear another name – his real name.

For the Kittewas believe that it is death for anyone but themselves to know their real name. This they keep to themselves and use a second name by which their tribe would know them.

The name, announced loudly by the toothless old medicine man, was White Knife.

It stopped the talk among the warriors when they heard that name, and they looked sharply towards the medicine man. In their minds was a suspicion, and they were shocked at it.

They listened, their copper faces grim in the red light, as the medicine man came, in his recital, to The Task.

When a youth had survived the warrior ordeal he was given a task to perform. That task was always to go out and bring in the scalp of an enemy. Now the warriors had a suspicion as to the identity of that enemy.

They were right in their suspicions. They heard the medicine man shout stridently: 'O White Knife,

8

listen unto my words. Heed them, for they direct you to your task. Go thou to the enemy named and get his scalp that it might decorate my lodge and bring safety to the tribe during winter.'

His skinny arm came rising up from the dried pelts and snake-skins and torn wings of birds that were his clothing. A finger pointed commandingly towards the dark edge of the menacingly silent forest.

'Go,' he ordered. 'Go to the village of the white men. But do not bring me back the scalp of any white man save that of our deadliest enemy. That I want – the scalp lock of He-Who-Is-Always-Tired – the white man whose name is Oak-o-Nur!'

It was while he was speaking that a curious thing happened. That shadow came up suddenly, noiselessly, from the forest edge. One moment the shadow was under the trees; the next it was up with the standing Kittewa warriors.

And the next it was gliding between their astonished ranks, and it was no longer a shadow but a man.

The women by the distant tipis saw it first and their shrill cries testified to the terror it brought to their wild hearts. For without telling, they knew him to be the feared enemy of the Kittewas.

The Kittewas had many enemies. In fact, every man was their enemy except the tribes of the Sioux, with whom they had kinship and who had to harbour them and give them protection when they needed it.

The Sioux were not proud of their Kittewa brethren and grew restive whenever their shadows darkened their lodge doors. For the Kittewas were the horse-stealers, the mischief-makers, the liars and the cheats and the cause of trouble between tribes and men. They were forever bringing outraged enemies upon them, and then they would flee into the hunting grounds of the mighty Sioux nation and demand shelter and even ask for aid to beat back their enemies.

And because they were brothers in blood, the Sioux tribes did as they were asked, though their hearts were against it.

So the Kittewa were hated by the proud Cheyenne as cowardly runaway dogs, and by the Arapaho and Chippeway as thieves and rascals. These tribes especially were feared by the cunning Kittewa, yet this fear was as nothing compared with the terror they bore for the man who carried the name of Oak-o-Nur, He-Who-Is-Always-Tired.

Oak-o-Nur.

That man, who had passed so swiftly, so unexpectedly, through the astonished ranks of Indians, paused on the edge of the fire at the sound of that name.

'O'Connor?' he drawled. Only then did the medicine man become aware of his presence. The masked face came twisting round, the sharp little eyes incredulous and yet filled with instant hate.

The man named O'Connor braced his legs apart, the warmth of the leaping fire on his back, as comfortable as a man before his own fireplace. Every Indian's eyes were upon him.

They saw a man bigger than the biggest brave among them, and the Kittewa are noted for the tallness of their warriors. He was truly a giant, this white man with his back to the fire. They noted the width of those mighty shoulders, saw the tightness of the faded blue shirt-sleeves where biceps bulged.

They saw and noted the slim hips of the true athlete, with the sagging ammunition belt upon which were holstered twin Colts with well-worn handles.

A big man, this O'Connor. A man careless in his appearance, anyone would have said. For his faded blue shirt was bereft of buttons so that it lay open on his barrel-like hairy chest unable apparently to bridge the last few inches. And his jeans, neither leg of which was tucked into his riding boots, were soiled and torn in a dozen places.

But few had more than a passing glance for the intruder's attire. They were looking at that fighting face under the pushed-back, sweat-stained old hat.

It was a face as bronzed as their own. A massive face, broad-boned and muscled in the manner of a prizefighter's. A battered, cheerfully ugly face, and yet even now filled with a kind of lazy good humour.

But the narrowed grey eyes, for all their casualness, didn't miss a thing. He saw, for instance, the swift movement of the medicine man's hand – saw the youth lurch away from the bonds that held him to the stake and knew he was free.

O'Connor spoke. His was a drawling, ironical voice as the Kittewa lingo fell from his tongue. It seemed to challenge the rigid, unmoving warriors, to mock at them, and yet even now not one of them moved. Such was the power of this man whom they

11

feared above all other enemies.

O'Connor said: 'So you want the scalp of He-Who-Is-Always-Tired, huh? You would like my hair decorating the buffalo hides of your home, O Man of Evil Medicine.'

He shifted and drew out a tobacco sack and deftly began to roll a cigarette. His eyes were cold as they looked towards the medicine man. The old man was quietly pushing White Knife, the new warrior, towards the big white man.

O'Connor said, suddenly, his voice rasping and hard, 'You hold on with your pushin' there!'

The big Texan paused in the act of licking his cigarette paper. His eyes were like cold steel.

'It's a fine medicine man you are, pickin' a kid to do your dirty work,' his ironical Irish-lilting voice rang out and the medicine man must have known some English, for he understood. Behind that carved and evil mask the eyes spat poison towards the big white man.

There was a little murmur and a movement among those Indians surrounding the Texan by the fire. They were the enemy of the white man, and yet O'Connor's sharp ears were quick to detect a murmur which was almost in sympathy with what he had said.

As if there were Indians among the Kittewas who objected also to a newly-initiated warrior being given this terrible task of striking down the tribe's most feared enemy.

O'Connor was thinking. 'I reckon some of these Injuns are fair enough, an' they opine that killin' me is a man's job, an' not one for a new kid.'

His eyes flickered swiftly round from one impassive fire-reddened Indian face to another. He didn't expect to find friends among them for all this little murmur and stir of approval. But he didn't reckon to lose his scalp to any of them, either.

The suddenness of his appearance had so startled everyone except the medicine man that as yet no move had been made towards the lone intruder. They couldn't believe that their most deadly enemy should have walked in among them in this manner unless there was more to it than they could see at that moment.

O'Connor saw heads turn uneasily and look into the darkness, and he knew what was in those Indian minds. They were sure that the darkness must contain an army of O'Connor's friends for him to venture so boldly into their midst.

But O'Connor knew he had no friends in that darkness. He didn't need friends, he told himself with a kind of grim humour. He was playing a bold hand and he reckoned he could win through.

But the medicine man had other ideas.

He was behind White Knife, the new Kittewa warrior. He was whispering fiercely, urgently into the young brave's ear. O'Connor couldn't hear the words, but he could guess what was being said.

'This was to be your task, O White Knife,' the medicine man would be whispering swiftly. 'He has walked right into your hands! Go thou and kill him and get his scalp, and then truly you will be lauded above all men in your tribe!'

There was a second's pause as White Knife crouched, the weariness gone from his young face as he stared at his mighty enemy silhouetted against the fire.

'And think, O Warrior,' went on the cunning medicine man, whose eyes had seen everything about that camp, and who knew just what to say to get men to do his bidding. 'Think that at this moment Gentle Fawn stands in those shadows, watching you. Think of her pride when she sees you holding aloft the scalp of this man whom we have such reason to hate.'

The medicine man's cunning words galvanised the youth into action. Gentle Fawn was watching. Gentle Fawn was to be his the moment he was a fully-fledged warrior!

Recklessly the young brave hurled himself forward, steel glinting ominously red in that firelight, as his tomahawk swung back preparatory to a death stroke.

White Knife was tall and lean, sinewy but strong. He came bounding in with the agility of a mountain deer.

And it looked so easy. That giant of a man seemed slow-moving, seemed slow-thinking by the look of that lazy expression on his big, battered face.

In those few hurtling strides towards O'Connor there was even a moment's surprise in White Knife's mind. He couldn't understand why this big lazy-looking man should have earned himself such a reputation with his tribe. Why, it was so easy for a swift tomahawk to find its way into that big body.

O'Connor wasn't there when the tomahawk arrived.

14

He moved and he didn't appear to move with any great haste. Yet somehow White Knife's tomahawk cut the air a good yard away from where the target had been a fraction of a second before.

More, White Knife found his wrist gripped as he plunged by. A steel clamp seemed to encircle that tomahawk-holding wrist. It was just one hand, but there was a pressure within those great bronzed fingers that was something beyond ordinary men.

A surge of pain went through that young Indian's arm as he felt himself being lifted off the ground by that mighty grip. His startled face looked within inches into the eyes of O'Connor. He expected to see hatred and deadly animosity. Because that is what you expect to see on the face of a man whose life you would have taken.

And he expected all in that instant to be riddled with shot from one of those heavy Colts.

Yet it wasn't like that at all. He looked into grey eyes that seemed if anything a little weary of what was happening. But there was no hatred in them. They just looked at him, and the Indian couldn't read the expression in those grey depths.

And those Colts remained in their holsters.

There was a twitch of the big white man's arm. It seemed effortless, and yet such was the strength in those mighty forearms that White Knife found himself being hurled away on to the ground, and in that same moment the tomahawk fell from his nerveless grip.

Astonished, ashamed of what had been done to him in public, and yet with it all relieved that he was still alive, White Knife crouched panting on the floor and looked up at his big enemy so close to the fire. Then his eyes went towards that tomahawk that lay in the dust.

O'Connor saw that glance, and in that same moment his hand sought a knife in his belt.

There was a gasp from the crowd of Indians as they saw O'Connor's hand leap forward with that knife point directed towards the fallen White Knife.

By the tipis a girl cried out in alarm, and then the cry broke off, as if hands had gone in horror to cover her open mouth.

But the knife fell in the dust only a few inches from the extended hand of the fallen brave. The Kittewas relaxed. This man had had no evil in his heart for the fallen White Knife.

They heard O'Connor speaking in that drawling voice of his now, and he was using the Dakota tongue which formed the basis of the Kittewa language. So they all understood him.

He was saying, 'There is a man's knife, O White Knife. Such a knife the white man makes, and it is sharp and keen and unlike those rusty blades of yours.'

For the knife that was within grasping distance of the Kittewa warrior was a gleaming thing of fine Spanish steel – a dagger with a wondrously ornamented handle. A trophy from the Mexican wars, though they did not know it.

O'Connor's voice was challenging. Legs braced apart, his chest almost bared towards his enemy, O'Connor shouted. 'But even the finest steel cannot take the life of Oak-O-Nor,' he thundered. 'Come, my young Kittewa friend, and plunge that knife right into my heart!'

Now he was holding his shirt wide apart, so that the hairy chest was exposed nakedly towards White Knife.

A roar went up from the Indians, but it was a roar of astonishment rather than an injunction for White Knife to do as he was bidden. But the medicine man's cackling, evil voice shouted instructions.

'Get thou that knife and take the heart and liver out of this accursed white man!'

White Knife was on his feet in a flash, that knife gripped fiercely in his lean brown fingers. His black shining eyes fastened upon the spot where he knew the white man's heart to be. And he knew that no man's skin was proof against the sharpness of a knife such as this.

With all his might he lunged forward, his arm swinging, and this time the white man stayed there, never moving, not for one instant covering that naked chest.

There was a gasp from the spectators as they saw the knife strike into the chest of the intruder. For one second they saw Indian and white man standing together, their eyes looking at each other, locked.

And then O'Connor pushed out with his hand and sent the young warrior reeling back.

And there was no blood on the knife that was withdrawn, and there was no mark on that broad chest – no fatal wound, no sign of blood!

TWO

'MIND READER.'

At that the Indians stood rigid, their eyes looking in fascination from dagger to the white man's chest. This truly was medicine beyond anything they had witnessed before!

O'Connor swung round on them. They saw those grey eyes under the battered brim of that disgraceful old hat, and they fell back in horror. For no man could have suffered such a knife wound and live.

It was in that moment that O'Connor seized his opportunity. He had those Indians silent and at his mercy for the moment. Such was their dread of the supernatural.

So he lifted his arms and he spoke to them as a friend.

'O Kittewas, listen unto my voice!' he called. 'I am the enemy of the Kittewas. That you have told me and others many times. And yet I would not be your enemy. I would that I were your friend, for I would

18

counsel you in ways that are to your advantage.'

It was doubtful if those Kittewas even heard him. They were still looking at the man who had been stabbed to the heart and yet lived – and bore not even a mark as a result of the assault.

But O'Connor went on: 'Always my tongue has spoken words of wisdom for you to heed, O Kittewas. When you would go to war because the white man's iron horse came across your hunting grounds, I told you no. I warned you that the fire-sticks of the pale-face would empty your lodges and the best thing for you was to accept presents in recompense for the land you had lost.'

O'Connor was thinking of that advice he had given at a parley of the Kittewa chieftains a year ago. They had appeared to accept it then.

They had taken the white man's gifts and promised friendship and safety for the engineers building the railroad.

But, even so, they had consistently attacked the railroad workers. Not boldly and openly as Cheyennes or Arapaho would have done. But stealthily, setting ambushes to wipe out small parties.

And, too, they had torn down the telegraph poles and wires that accompanied the building of the railroad almost as fast as they were put up. Not a man in the Kittewa tribe but had ornaments of copper made from the white man's telegraph wire.

Now, O'Connor said: 'We have had enough of your marauding. If there is any more trouble, the white man will descend upon you and burn your villages and drive you right out of your hunting grounds.

That is a promise,' he said with determination.

At that a chieftain, trembling with passion, stepped forward and pointed a hooked finger at the white man who had the temerity to stand in their midst and speak to them thus.

'Always it is the red man!' he shouted with ire. 'But you do not speak, O white man, of the many Kittewa braves who are now with the Great Spirit as the result of your guns.'

O'Connor's voice snapped back: 'Sure, there's quite a few Kittewas who won't go on marauding expeditions. They got theirs when they tried to wipe out the railroad workers.' His eyes were hard and unmoved. He said: 'They should have thought of that before tryin' to get white men's scalps!'

But that chieftain was not there to argue on logic. To him the Kittewa was always right and the white man always wrong. Now he shouted again: 'Always it is you, O white man, who defeats our warriors in battle. Always our wounded return and say that Oak-O-Nor was in the party that defeated them.'

That was true. O'Connor had taken to riding as escort with working parties far away from the base camp. And his knowledge of Indian tactics, combined with his accurate marksmanship, had resulted in many an ambusher being in turn ambushed. The fame of Careless O'Connor had spread far and wide among the Kittewa tribesmen.

But remembering those defeats, the Kittewa braves now thronged forward angrily, close on two hundred of them, all intent on ending the life of this man who had defeated the Kittewa so often.

O'Connor saw flashing eyes and faces that were flushed with passion. He saw hands gripping weapons and knew that he had little time in which to act if he intended to save himself.

He acted. The new young warrior, White Knife, had crept away, disgraced at his overthrow in public. That was more than the young warrior could bear.

But the knife he had used – the knife that O'Connor had so contemptuously tossed across to him – was lying on the ground.

Now O'Connor ambled across and picked it up. The moment his hand closed upon that knife, the big Texan leapt forward and seized the astonished medicine man before he had time to move.

O'Connor's big hand gripped that skinny neck under the greasy black hair. He dragged the medicine man round, so that his body was between the Texan and the oncoming mass of Indians.

The Indians halted. They saw a knife held to the neck of their medicine man – this man who was feared and worshipped even more than their tribal chieftains.

They heard O'Connor's ironical voice call out: 'Mebbe your medicine man would like to show he c'n survive dagger blows like I did!'

He let the point of that dagger bite into the skin of that medicine man's neck. The medicine man panicked.

He screamed, terrified at what he thought was imminent death. The knife was hurting him. He tried to pull away, but he was helpless in the grip of the big Texan.

Big O'Connor, his face grim for all that there was a touch of humour on his words, twisted that evil masked face so that he could look into the frightened eyes of the medicine man. The dagger was held close to the windpipe now.

O'Connor drawled: 'I figger you don't like cold steel, my friend.' His eyes lifted swiftly to where the Indians had paused irresolutely. 'Better tell your amigos to hold their hosses!' he advised grimly. 'Ef them varmints come a step nearer, by glory I'll slit your throat for you!'

O'Connor felt the medicine man gulp. Then a high-pitched, shrieking voice called out urgently to the Indians: 'Keep back, or this mad white man will kill me!' The medicine man shouted in terror. That knife-point on his windpipe was certainly terrifying enough.

Now again O'Connor spoke to them.

'I will give you more advice, amigos. Listen not to the words of troublemakers like your medicine man. When they tell you to attack the white man and destroy his property, they give you bad advice. But then they are evil men, and can only bring trouble on the tribe.

'Your medicine man is behind most of the trouble, we know. That is why I have come to you tonight, risking my life to do so. I have come to tell you to throw out this medicine man and his friends from the tribe, and I tell you now that you will grow fat and rich if you will accept the white man's presents and not attack the railroad that is being laid across your territory.'

Suddenly, as if he were tired of talking gently and peaceably to these people, it seemed as if a gust of anger swept over him. His mighty arm shook the medicine man until his teeth rattled in his ancient head.

'Why, goldarn it, he ain't even a proper medicine man!' he exploded. 'Listen to my voice, O Kittewas. I, too, know magic, but it is good medicine and not bad medicine such as this man performs for you.'

Someone fell into the trap. It was that same Indian chief who had shown such anger a few minutes ago. Now, still shaking with rage, but not daring to advance in case the medicine man was dispatched before their eyes, he shouted: 'Show us your magic, then!'

O'Connor asked: 'Haven't I shown you enough?' That silenced most of the murmurs that had arisen at the chief's words. Truly it was not every day they saw a man stabbed to the heart and yet live.

But the chief called: 'That was a trick. Always every man knows one trick. But let us see real magic, and then we might believe you when you say that our medicine man is not a good one!'

O'Connor was waiting for just that challenge. Now he called out: 'Listen to my words. I can see into the minds of men. I can read their thoughts and know what they are thinking.

'Let me tell you what was in the mind of the medicine man only a few minutes ago. He gave unto White Knife his real name, didn't he? That name I know!'

This statement produced an astonishing effect

upon the medicine man. His head came twisting round so that those eyes behind the mask were looking incredulously at the big Texan. Truly if O'Connor knew that name – a name known only to the medicine man and White Knife – then O'Connor was above all other men and did know magic. That was the reasoning of a medicine man who knew that all his own medicine was just so many tricks.

O'Connor nodded confidently, 'I will give you that name, the real name of White Knife.' He paused dramatically and then shouted, 'The real name is – Ta-ny-Ta – Leaping Deer!'

There was no need to ask the medicine man if that name was correct. His legs seemed to buckle underneath him so that he almost fell out of O'Connor's grasp. Incredulously those Indians looked from the medicine man to the big white man whose knife was still pressed against the skinny throat. This was magic beyond anything they had seen before. O'Connor could read a man's mind!

O'Connor was moving now. He had come all this way to warn the Kittewa about their behaviour and to threaten them with reprisals if they did not mend their ways. And he had upset their evil medicine man, with his bad advice that kept the tribe plundering and pillaging when they might have been living in harmony with the white man.

Now he wanted to go and he intended to go unhurriedly and in safety. The medicine man was a guarantee of the latter.

While the medicine man was a prisoner with that

knife ready to slit his throat, O'Connor knew that no one would attack him.

So, as calmly as if he were leaving the bunkhouse back in his native Texas, O'Connor began to walk through those parting ranks of hostile, sullen Indians, the medicine man being propelled before him.

They wanted to use their weapons on him, those Indians, but while that knife was pressed against the neck of their medicine man not a hand was raised against the bold white man. O'Connor, a confident grin on his big, battered face, ambled towards the outer ring of darkness, beyond the firelight where his horse was patiently awaiting him.

Crazy Elk, the angry-looking Indian chief, could not contain himself at sight of their deadly enemy walking out of their grasp so easily. Perhaps he cared little for the life of the medicine man anyway.

At any rate, out of the corner of his eye, O'Connor caught a swift movement as the Indian chief suddenly swung a tomahawk back and then hurled it towards the big Westerner. It would have brained Careless if it had reached him. And if he had ducked it would have bruised the hapless medicine man, and that wouldn't have suited O'Connor's purpose either.

For with the medicine man dead the whole tribe would set on him.

For one second O'Connor released his hold on that scrawny neck. In that same second his hand flashed down to his worn gun butt.

The whole movement was too fast for those

Indians to see in that uncertain firelight. All they knew was that one moment a tomahawk was hurtling through the air towards the paleface; the next the thundering bark of a Colt was heard and the axe was shattered in full flight.

Stupefied, Crazy Elk looked at the pieces of the polished stone tomahawk that lay on the ground. His eyes lifted. Smoke was blowing away from the vicinity of the big Westerner.

But now there was no gun in his hand. Once again the medicine man was grasped firmly by the neck and was being trundled unwillingly towards the darkness.

That put a stop to any more ideas on attacking him. The Indian warriors had seen enough that night not to want to seek out individual combat with this formidable white man!

So they stood, fuming and raging, while O'Connor marched his prisoner steadily away.

They were going through the tipis, where a few cooking fires threw up a flickering light.

At sight of him, the womenfolk screamed shrilly and gathered their children and ran to shelter into their smoke-blackened lodges. It made O'Connor grin to see them run away from him like that.

And then the grin was wiped from his face. Someone was barring their path. When he came nearer he realised that that person was – a girl.

THREE

'CARELESS' DOES A ROPE TRICK.

O'Connor halted, bringing the medicine man to a standstill at the same time. He saw wild but beautiful eyes in a high-cheekboned face. A dusky face, with a frame of black plaited hair. A lovely young face, O'Connor thought, and marvelled that such beauty could be found in a Kittewa camp.

He recognised the fear on that face, and then realised that something more than fear was causing that girl to stand before him and challenge him when no warrior in the tribe dared do it.

O'Connor didn't know the reason why just then. But Gentle Fawn had seen the warrior who was to have been her male humbled by this big white man, and she wanted to strike him down in some vain idea that it might help White Knife to regain his prestige as a warrior within the tribe.

For she had seen White Knife lope disconsolately, head bowed in shame, into the shadows. And she had known that he would not return to his tribe while the disgrace was upon him.

O'Connor called out sharply, in Kittewa, 'Out of my way, gal, I don't want to have to hurt a woman.' He marched his prisoner forward again, coming right up to the girl. She seemed to stumble sideways, as if in panic, and O'Connor breathed a sigh of relief.

He was going past the girl when she lashed out and her strong young fingers clasped around the wrist that held the knife against the medicine man's throat. She tried to drag the fist away.

She hadn't the strength to do it, but all the same she had the tenacity to hold on to O'Connor, and it was perplexing to the big Westerner. A man – he could have dealt with him, he thought grimly. But, tarnation, what did a galoot do to an Indian maiden, especially one as pretty as this?

The worst of it was that sight of the girl's courage brought the manhood back to those Indian warriors behind. There was a yell from someone's throat, and then they came streaming after the white man and his prisoner. In a second they would be surrounding him again, O'Connor realised, and this time he thought he might not get out of their midst quite so easily. Now the element of surprise had gone.

There was nothing else for it. O'Connor wasn't going to lose his life over a girl, but even so he wasn't going to strike her. That was against the code of the West.

The medicine man struck her instead. Not hard. Careless simply threw the medicine man and the girl together, wrenched his wrist free and broke into a run that was deceptive in its speed from so big a man.

But now the Indians, their throats exulting in a screaming war whoop, were right behind him.

O'Connor raced for the trees and reached them twenty yards ahead of the nearest warrior, just as the first arrow came speeding after him. Twenty yards – but in the darkness it was a good lead.

He crashed on towards where his horse had been left, and the Indians had to follow him by sound. That wasn't easy, but they kept close behind him, all the same.

By the time he'd run through that neck of trees, O'Connor had gained another twenty or thirty yards upon his nearest pursuer. As he ran out into open country beyond he could hear the panting of his enemies, their grunts and howls of dismay as they ran into trouble in the darkness. He could have opened fire with his Colts, but his concern was to save his skin and not damage the hide of anyone else.

He saw his horse, under the last of the trees, and any doubts that had been in his mind left him now. Once astride that big ungainly brute and he would leave his pursuers standing, he was thinking.

Just at that moment he heard the thunder of unshod hooves on hard-baked ground and his spirits immediately dropped. Some Indian had used his head – perhaps it was Crazy Elk, who looked a cunning, far-sighted Indian. Anyway, someone must have guessed that the interloper's horse must have been somewhere back of those woods, and they had immediately sprung upon bare-backed ponies and come riding to intercept him.

It made the pursuit closer than the big Texan liked.

He came vaulting over the haunches of his horse, clean into his saddle. The big beast immediately reared and then plunged forward as O'Connor dug his heels into the animal's hide. He came riding out into sudden moonlight, as a crescent moon came unexpectedly out from behind some low-hanging cloud. He was fanning his horse with his hat, turning to look over his shoulder at the same time.

He saw a bunch of Kittewa warriors, clearly revealed in that moonlight, urging their nimble-footed ponies into pursuit of him.

O'Connor stuck that old hat back on his head and dragged out his repeater from his saddle scabbard. Still he didn't like shooting. If necessary, he was prepared to shoot his way out of a difficulty, but he knew that, riding at that speed on that rough ground and with only moonlight to assist him, shooting was chancy.

He was riding now between stunted birch trees whose white trunks gleamed in ghostly fashion in the moonlight. It gave him an idea.

He grunted to himself, 'I ain't goin' lickety-split on this hoss for no pack of blamed Injuns. Might break my precious neck.'

Anyway, O'Connor wasn't the kind of man to exert himself if he could find a way of doing something more easily. He thought he'd found a way now.

He shook out his rope and rode bending forward in the saddle, his eyes seeking for a projecting stump of a branch on one of the birches. He saw it and his rope whirled above his head and then snaked towards that stunted tree. The noose looped – tightened and held.

Instantly O'Connor swung away, riding at right angles now to his original course. As he rode he paid out that rope until he was at the end of it. Dragging back on the bit, O'Connor halted his horse. With one lightning twist, O'Connor had the end of the rope around yet another birch tree. It was fastened.

Then O'Connor drove his heels into his horse's side, and went bounding forward on his original course. As he rode he looked back.

The Indians had swerved to follow him when he went off at a tangent, but now they came riding back along their original course, seeing him fleeing ahead of them.

In their lead was an Indian wearing the many-feathered bonnet of a chief. Grinning to himself, Careless hoped that this would be Crazy Elk.

It was. Crazy Elk, noted for his recklessness in battle, was a good thirty yards ahead of his followers. He was riding so fast that he never even saw the rope that stretched breast high in front of him. He never knew what hit him, either.

All the following Indians knew was that suddenly Crazy Elk's horse was riding on without him, while Crazy Elk hung suspended in curious manner in mid-air.

Crazy Elk found something like a mighty hand

31

clasping him across the chest. It was the rope, taut between two supple trees. The weight of his body dragged those trees in momentarily, and then they straightened, and the effect was as if Crazy Elk was caught on the string of a giant catapult.

Careless O'Connor, trotting his horse now, heard a dismal howl as a terrified Indian chieftain found himself being hurled backwards towards his followers.

He hit the nearest warrior and knocked him out of his saddle. That was enough to stop the charging Indians. All at once they remembered that this was night time and they did not like the darkness. And they remembered that the big white man had the power of making medicine.

They felt sure that this was more of the white man's magic, and they were afraid that if they continued it might be their turn to take bad medicine.

Even Crazy Elk had had enough. When he saw his dejected party of Indian braves he was only too ready to ride away from the scene of the mysterious occurrence.

O'Connor rode on a couple of miles, and then made camp for the night. Before dawn he was on his way again, however, riding eastwards towards a gap in the hills through which the white man's iron horse was being projected.

By noon he was riding alongside the new-laid track that came down from the hills. It was almost through Kittewa country now, but that didn't make the project any safer.

For the long unprotected line of track was all too

vulnerable to the attacks of the thieving, rascally Kittewa tribe.

It was rolling country here, with plenty of cover which had once given shelter to much game. But the hunters seeking meat to provision the track-layers had driven all four-footed creatures far away from the railroad. Now Careless did not expect anything living except maybe an Indian or two.

In this he was right, only coming upon a group of workers on the outskirts of the shanty town that was always erected at the end of the track.

It was along towards the end of a canyon where workers were slinging up more telegraph wires. They were working with their guns close to their side, and when they heard the advance of hooves towards them, all jumped for their weapons immediately. They faced round, their eyes suspicious until they were able to identify the lone rider.

Careless drew rein in their midst and a tight smile came to his face as he heard their sighs of relief. They put down their guns.

'You're kinder jumpy,' he drawled.

A lean man who had lost most of his teeth squinted quizzically at him and then said abruptly, 'Can you wonder, with them blamed Kittewa forever takin' pot shots at us?'

He spat far out into the canyon. Then his head jerked round again to look at big Careless O'Connor on that big ugly horse of his.

'You know what I'd do with them Kittewa?'

Careless shook his head, and yet he knew. He had heard this said by many men before.

'I'd fix up every man along this track with a Winchester and I'd go into that Kittewa territory an' I wouldn't stop until the last Kittewa was hangin' from a branch!'

There was a murmur of deep-throated approval at those sentiments. These men had had enough – had suffered quite sufficiently – at the hands of the Kittewa.

Big Careless put his leg across the saddle and idly rubbed his hairy calf for an instant while his eyes looked into the distance – and the future.

'Mebbe you're right at that,' he agreed. 'The only thing I c'n see agen that proceedin' is we want to get this line finished an' joined up with the Pacific section. We want a trans-Continental railroad!'

The man with few teeth was impatient. 'Ain't that what I'm sayin'?' he demanded irately. 'Looks like we're goin' to lose out ef we don't put a stop to them Kittewas. Lordy, we're weeks behind schedule now, an' that sure is costin' someone a packet of money.'

Again he spat into the canyon, and there was a viciousness about the action that wasn't lost on the keen-eyed Texan sitting his saddle above the linesmen.

'Wipe out the Kittewa an' we'd be able to get on with the job,' the man said impatiently, and again there was a growl of approval from the other linesmen.

This time Careless O'Connor spoke straight out. 'You'd not save this line by goin' for the Kittewa,' he said. 'Though that's just what I threatened the Kittewa we'll be doin' soon.'

He thumped the pommel of his saddle, 'Don't you see, we can't go an' rout out them Kittewa. They're blood brothers of the Sioux Nation, an' the moment we go after them they'll be away into Dakota territory. An' then if we follow we'll have a full-scale war on our hands – war agen the Sioux Nation!'

He didn't need to say more than that. Three times there had been war with the Sioux Nation, and in each except the last, the mighty Sioux warriors had defeated the white men in battle. The name of the Sioux people was feared and respected, and the thought of bringing them on to the line was enough to still the ready tongues of these workmen.

O'Connor rode on after that, but he was thinking of some of the things those linesmen had said. Especially he was thinking of those long delays, not always caused by Indians, which had set back the track-laying schedule and even threatened the ultimate success of the enterprise.

There were people in Washington already saying that it was too expensive to build a railroad through a wilderness. They were urging an abandonment of the project even before it linked up with the Pacific coast track-layers.

Then O'Connor rode through the dust into the village of huts that was the end of the track.

They were frame buildings, all of them. Mostly they were the hutments of the rail construction company, housing men and stores and equipment. But with these huts were gaming saloons, bars, and even a few cabarets, so-called.

Every few weeks the entire town was taken to

pieces, put on to flat cars and trundled up to the end of track, there to be erected again for a few more weeks until more track had been laid westward.

O'Connor hated the place. There were too many people, and too much brawling and unpleasantness. He liked the hills and the solitude and the freshness of life in the open.

But he had his report to make and now he swung off his horse outside the office of Joe Butcher, the construction boss.

He gave his horse to a boy to take round to a livery stable to be attended to, while he climbed the two steps that led into the office.

Butcher was sitting behind his desk, apparently studying the figures relating to the previous day's work.

He was a hard man who yet maintained a reputation for joviality among the men. He had red, weathered cheeks, and a heavy moustache that was going grey. He was a big man, with plenty of muscle behind his ears, as the Irish whom he controlled would say.

O'Connor didn't care much for the man. He was never sure of that hearty smile, because it seemed to him that the smile touched only Butcher's lips and not his eyes. He had a feeling that Butcher could be a mean man if he had the opportunity.

But Butcher was his boss for the moment. At any rate, it was to Butcher that he had to come with his report.

Butcher's face broke into a quick smile of welcome, and yet the eyes were hard and calculating as they looked at the Texan.

36

'You got back safe?' Butcher looked perhaps mildly surprised as he stated that fact.

O'Connor drawled: 'I figger you didn't expect to see me again.' He began to roll himself a cigarette.

Butcher mopped the sweat from his face with a white, spotted-red handkerchief. 'Yep. I figgered when you said you were goin' to talk to them Kittewas that mebbe I'd never see you agen. It's a crazy thing to think about, because I wouldn't trust them Kittewas anywhere.'

His massive fingers drummed the table. Abruptly he said; 'Of course, you changed your mind an' didn't go to the Kittewa village.'

He was so sure of his statement that he didn't make his remark a question. Therefore, his eyes widened when Careless shook his head.

'Nope. I said I was goin' to speak to them heathen Kittewas, an' that's just what I did.'

Before Butcher could recover from his surprise, Careless told Butcher all that had happened. When he had finished Butcher shook his head wonderingly.

'That's the kind of thing I could never do,' he said. 'I hate them Injuns, an' I wouldn't go near them, not if for a fortune.'

But there were things that puzzled the construction boss.

'That knife?' he said suddenly. 'I don't work that one out. How come you lived when that Injun knifed you?'

O'Connor smiled, and his hand went to his belt from which protruded a knife handle – the knife that he had thrown towards the prostrate White Knife back there at the Kittewa camp.

But when he pulled the knife from his belt there was no blade attached to the ornamental handle. That is, there was no blade for a second.

Then the big Texan must have touched a hidden spring, and the knife blade shot out with a click.

'A trick knife,' Butcher said in surprise. 'I've seen them things before.'

'You see plenty down along the Mexican border,' Careless answered easily. He was playing with the knife, holding the point against the table top and pressing on the handle. The blade each time disappeared backwards into the handle.

Then O'Connor said suddenly: 'I guess it was lucky for me them Injuns had never seen this kind of knife before. If they'd found this other spring—'

He shrugged. His finger touched a little metal button and pressed it in. This time when he threw the knife on to the trestle table the blade stuck half-an-inch deep into the rough wood. Now the blade was locked and could not recede under pressure into the handle.

Butcher said grudgingly: 'You took a risk. You've got a nerve, O'Connor. I wish I had nerve like yours.'

O'Connor said: 'I figgered I could get away with it, an' I did. I reckoned that if I could impress them Kittewas I might get them to see sense and keep away from the railroad.'

Wrathfully he slapped his thigh.

'It's that darned medicine man,' he said angrily. 'He's bad medicine for the tribe, an' keeps 'em agen the white man. I'd like to have brought him out with me an' got him tried by the military. After all, them Kittewas took presents an' broke their treaty with us.'

But Butcher still had questions to ask.

He leaned forward, and said: 'There's one thing you still haven't explained, O'Connor. And that is how come you knew the real name that had just been given to White Knife by the medicine man?'

O'Connor let his eyes come slowly round until they looked at that thick-set construction boss. And then slowly he asked a surprising question: 'Ever remember a railroad engineer called Cal Menzies?'

At the mention of the name for one second those big, strong fingers of the construction boss ceased to tap upon the rough trestle table top.

And for just one second the heavy moustached face seemed to go rigid with shock.

But when Joe Butcher lifted his eyes to meet those of the lounging, drawling Texan it was to see Careless gazing apparently innocently out through the open doorway. Joe Butcher stirred.

'Cal Menzies? Yeh, I know Cal. It was too bad about Cal.'

'Yeh. It was too bad for Cal.' O'Connor played with the rim of his old hat. 'Cal was a friend of mine. He was second in command on a construction job down Santa Fe.'

Joe Butcher nodded impatiently. 'I was in charge of that railroad construction project,' he said.

It seemed almost as if Joe Butcher did not want to talk about Cal Menzies. But the drawling voice continued.

'They were behind schedule on the Santa Fe line,

39

too. It's queer how you get yourself jobs an' always seem to fall behind schedule,' the Texan drawled ironically.

'Meanin'?' Just a slight movement of Butcher's hand – towards the gun strapped round his waist. But O'Connor was still looking out through the door and apparently oblivious of the momentary threat.

'Cal did everythin' he could to catch up time, but one durned thing after another slowed them up. Then came the worst disaster of all.

'They were needin' explosives to get through a rocky barrier, an' goldarn it, somehow them explosives never seemed to get up to them. Always they were bein' shunted to some other place.

'So Cal rode back to the marshalin' yards an' hitched on an engine to the dynamite trucks an' started to pull 'em out to the end of the track himself.'

Butcher was drumming again on the table. His eyes could just be seen peering through his bushy eyebrows. He nodded. 'You don't need to go on. I know that story all too well. It bust that railroad project and now that railroad don't go anywhere. It's just another line that ends in the desert.'

'Waitin',' said O'Connor softly, 'for some other company to finish it off.'

Butcher said, his voice suddenly harsh: 'Injuns attacked that powder train, an' it never got through. That was the end of the Santa Fe railroad.'

O'Connor got to his feet, and he looked mighty big inside that low-ceilinged shack.

'Yeh,' he said softly. 'There were Injuns waitin' up

the track. Almost as if someone had put them there,' he said significantly. 'They rode alongside that train, an' it couldn't move fast because of the dangerous freight.

'Then Injuns opened up with fire arrows an' set one of the trucks on fire.'

His eyes came round to meet those of the construction boss.

'Ever heard of Injuns doin' such a darned thing before, Butcher?' he rapped.

That had puzzled O'Connor ever since he had been sent down at the complaint of shareholders following the disaster which had ended the Santa Fe project.

Indians did foolish things, just as other men did, but he had never heard of them deliberately setting fire to a train of freight cars before. Always an Indian wanted loot before destruction, and this was plain, downright destruction without prospect of loot right from the start.

'It was almost as if they knew there were explosives aboard and they wanted to blow it up,' O'Connor continued. 'Cal saw all of this from the cab with the driver and fireman. He was firin' with a Winchester, but agen that red horde it was as good as a peashooter only.

'Suddenly one of the trucks blew up, and then the next truck was on fire. So they went crazily across the desert. They were dragging a flaming train of cars, and one by one they were losing them as they went up in explosions. The Injuns had pulled away when they saw the train on fire. They'd done their work well – whatever that work was.'

Butcher rose now, and there was something threat-ening in the way he stood there, not as tall as O'Connor, but perhaps heavier because of the beef on his shoulders. His harsh voice rasped: 'That train never got through. It all went up suddenly.'

O'Connor nodded. 'Yeh, it all went up. Suddenly, just when Cal was hopin' to pull at least a few wagons out to safety, the whole lot went up in flames. It tore up the track an' threw the engine into the desert.

'In the town they'd heard the explosions and were ridin' out to investigate. They found poor Cal alive. He was terribly injured by that explosion, and it was weeks before they knew he would survive that ordeal.

'I got the story from Cal,' O'Connor said. 'That was after the railroad was abandoned and you had come north to take charge of this new project, Butcher.'

Butcher said: 'How could Cal Menzies speak to you when he had no voice left?'

'Sure, that was true enough. The explosion destroyed Cal's powers of speech and left him deaf into the bargain. Poor Cal, but all the same he told me what had happened. I just watched his lips and in time I could tell what he was saying.'

'Lip readin'.' Butcher was surprised at that.

'Sure. I got pretty good at lip readin', an' tonight it paid off well.'

'You mean,' said Butcher quickly, 'you lip-read the medicine man when he was givin' White Knife his real name?'

But O'Connor shook his head. 'Not quite. That

medicine man wore the usual ceremonial mask. I couldn't see his lips.'

Careless was suddenly wishing that he had torn that mask off the medicine man. It would have been a dangerous thing to do, but O'Connor would have liked to have seen the face of that malevolent little man who controlled the destinies of the Kittewa tribe. But there had been no time.

'But I was in the shadows, watchin' the face of that young Injun fastened to the stake. You know what happens when somethin' important is said to you. You repeat it, don't you? Waal, White Knife repeated his own name after the medicine man had whispered in his ear. Ta-ny-Ta, I saw his lips say. It was easy!'

Butcher made an attempt to be jovial again. 'It sure paid off, O'Connor. It certainly made them Injuns think you were a man of powerful medicine.'

'It was luck,' O'Connor said. 'But then I've always gambled on luck, and it seems to have paid off all the time.'

O'Connor walked to the door and his big body was for the moment silhouetted against the fierce prairie sunlight. Just for one second there came an impulse to Joe Butcher to shoot him in the back.

For one moment Butcher knew that here was a man who might threaten his safety. But then Butcher relaxed. It would have been unwise to have shot O'Connor in the back.

O'Connor was too important a man to be killed out of hand and nothing happen. This big, ambling mountain of a man had a reputation known through-out the American continent. He was a special agent of the Federal Government. Whenever there were frontier troubles, Careless O'Connor was sent to sort them out.

As now, for instance. Federal money had been poured into this trans-Continental railroad project, and it wasn't going well. Delays which were causing the engineers to fall down on their schedules were imperilling the people against this idea, mainly to discredit the visionaries who had conceived it and who were the political bosses of the moment. They were trying to stop this railroad project, and it seemed as though Fate was playing into their hands.

But in the past few weeks O'Connor had been put on the job of trouble-busting. Whenever there was a complication, the Federal agent went riding out to eliminate it.

Since O'Connor had been assigned to this project, it had gone through at greater speed, and already they were catching up on lost time. He was a powerful man, with the whole weight of the Federal Government behind him.

So Joe Butcher's gun stayed in his holster.

O'Connor said: 'I'll be seein' you, Butcher. I want to ride out to where the men are workin'. They're movin' out of Kittewa territory now, into Dakota land.'

With that remark, which seemed to be without significance, O'Connor went striding off through the dust towards the livery stable.

Joe Butcher followed him to the door. And then he mounted his horse and rode out along the railroad to where his men were working. As he rode he was mentally selecting the men he needed for a special job. That job was to eliminate Federal-agent Careless O'Connor from the scene!

For Butcher, for the first time, realised that O'Connor had direct suspicions against him, was already on to the fact that he, Joe Butcher, was sabotaging this trans-Continental railroad project, just as he had been paid to sabotage the Santa Fe railroad months earlier.

FOUR

'A TOMAHAWK IN THE NIGHT.'

It was evening when Careless rode back into the town. He had been uneasy, and had wanted to be up forward where the railroad workers were laying the rusty new lines that came by the hundred on the flat freight cars.

Out there in the blazing heat of the sun, with close on a thousand men sweating and toiling to lay sleepers and drag up the rails at the double and spike them in, amid the welter of sound as hammers clanged on metal and men shouted hoarse instructions to each other, the uneasiness had not left him.

He had a sense of impending disaster and when the boss ganger came and told him jubilantly that they were five hundred yards ahead of schedule in the past thirty-six hours, he still could not raise a smile. That boss ganger was a new friend of his, but a

46

good one. He was another Irishman, Tom Riordan. Tom was as tough as they came, ugly and forbidding in appearance, with a voice that could frighten the hide off a bull and yet underneath was as friendly a spirit as any man could meet.

And Tom after his first greeting, looking round to see that the work was still going on at an almost frenzied pace, Tom had a warning to give Careless.

He spat on the ground. 'I saw that Joe Butcher come ridin' up ahead of you, Careless,' he told him.

Careless' eyes narrowed. 'He got in ahead of me?' The last he had seen of Joe Butcher was back in that office. The fellow must have ridden hell for leather to get out here ahead of him, because Careless hadn't come slowly himself.

'Yeh. He got here and straightway he went into a huddle with some of his huckster pals.'

O'Connor nodded, knowing who they would be. These were other ganger foremen, picked for their jobs by Joe Butcher because of their toughness and their ability to handle a mob of unruly Irishers.

Tom came out into the open then. 'I heard your name mentioned when I came past the group. It looked like Joe Butcher was talkin' about you, an' I didn't like the way they were lookin'. They're a mean lot of huskies, them gangers of Joe's.'

O'Connor's eyes met the boss ganger's levelly. 'You think Joe Butcher's goin' to fix trouble for me?'

Tom shrugged. 'I don't rightly know what to think. All I know is, your name was on his lips when I passed, an' he looked like he could murder you.'

O'Connor said gently: 'Thanks for the warnin',

47

pal. Mebbe Joe Butcher would like to murder me.'

He was thinking that mention of Cal Menzies' name had been a warning to Joe Butcher. All he had at the moment was suspicion, but to a man like Butcher it was sufficient to act upon suspicion.

O'Connor's hands slapped the holsters of his guns. 'If Joe Butcher wants trouble, he won't find me runnin' away,' he said unpleasantly.

The Irish face of Tom Riordan broke into a grin. 'That's what I thought I'd hear from you, you old spalpeen,' he said. And then he added: 'But if you get into trouble, Careless, just shout out for Tom Riordan. I've got plenty tough friends layin' them rails now, an' if I give the word they'll come a-runnin' to help you.'

It was O'Connor's turn to grin. He could just imagine the alacrity with which Tom Riordan's fighting Irishers would down tools to join in a scrap. All the same, it was good to know he had friends.

He rode off after that, circling the newly surveyed section along which the track was being laid. All the way up men lifted their heads and shouted to him, recognising him. He was a favourite with these tough men who worked so far away from civilisation.

And these men realised, too, that in the past few weeks this big fighting Texan had quite often stood between them and danger from the sneaking, rascally Kittewas.

One of them shouted: 'You can go home now, you careless critter!'

O'Connor reined in his horse and grinned expectantly. The fellow leaned on the peavey with which he

48

was turning the rails dropped from the flat cars.

He squinted up at O'Connor on his horse, and said: 'We're right out of Kittewa country now. I figger we're into safety at last.'

Big Careless looked back along the line, beyond the shack town already two miles behind the end of the track. And beyond that was the canyon which led into the heart of the Kittewa country. He could not find relief in his own mind that they were out of that hilly, forest fastness.

'Brother,' he said softly, 'I wish I could feel like you do!'

Now as he rode into the town he was thinking that the danger was still there. It was impossible to police every yard of that track that ran into the Kittewa hills, and at any time it was vulnerable and open to savage attacks. He wondered what would happen when the first trains came through that were not crowded with husky railroad construction men, all armed to the teeth.

And then his eyes went over his shoulder and he looked westward into the lands of the Dakota, the most powerful tribe in the Sioux Nation.

He was thinking: 'They're a proud people. An' fine fighters. I hope to heck nothin' happens to bring them on the warpath agen us.'

With the Sioux Nation out on the war trails, progress would be completely stopped. It wouldn't be like the attacks of the Kittewa, those few miserable nuisances by comparison.

Then Careless forgot that worry. He was a tired man from over twenty-four hours on the trail. There was nothing he could do now except hit the hay-bag and grab some sleep.

He left his horse in the livery stable and slowly walked round to the saloon where in the tiniest room at the back he had a narrow bunk bed that was merely a shelf of planks set against the wall. But to the tough Westerner it was as comfortable as the finest feather bed back east.

He had to go through the saloon and into a passage that led to his room. None of these buildings stood more than one floor high, because they had to be pulled down in a matter of hours, transported a few miles and then erected again, all on the same day.

He was off his guard. It must have been the tiredness that made him for once live up to his name. Though it was unusual for him to be careless when real danger threatened.

As he walked down that narrow passage he saw a man lurching towards him. Careless stood aside to let him pass. In that same instant he realised that a door was opening, the one next to his own room.

All at once suspicion flooded over him.

For he had seen a face in that opening, shadowy doorway. He didn't recognise it, but it was an evil face, unwashed and unshaven, and the eyes were curiously, glittering bright.

It was those eyes that gave Careless his warning. He had seen eyes glittering like that before, and always it was when a man was in the mood to kill another.

He brought his hand round towards his guns. Then he halted within an inch of their butts. For something hard was pressing into his back.

He realised in a fraction of a second that that man

lurching past him had whipped out his gun and had him covered from the rear.

The other man came out of that doorway, and he, too, came up with a heavy Colt.

O'Connor grated, 'What's the idea? You get that gun out of my back or I'll knock your blamed heads off.'

The man who had first drawn on him shoved hard, and that got Careless moving down the passage. 'You won't knock anybody's head off,' the man grunted, and Careless got the smell of liquor from the man's breath.

Plainly these two hucksters had been filling themselves with courage while awaiting his return.

Careless' thoughts flew swiftly to the warning Tom Riordan had given him. He knew without telling that these men had been planted on him by Joe Butcher. Joe was pretty near to the truth as to why a crack Federal agent should have been sent down here to the trans-Continental railroad.

The man with the gun shoved hard again and said, 'You walk right out through that back door an' keep walking.'

Careless didn't hurry. He had an idea what was waiting for him out there in the gathering dusk.

Over his shoulder he flung back, 'You want me to walk into the mesquite away from the town, huh? Then I reckon you're goin' to put a bullet through the back of my head. Yeh?'

The man behind him was grinning wolfishly. This, after all, was easy. He and his crony hadn't thought it would be easy to do away with the big Texan, but he was no trouble at all, seemingly.

It made the two gunmen swell up with pride. One of them said, 'He's a good guesser, this fellar. Reckon we'll do just as he says, then he'll die knowin' he was right at least once in his life.'

The two men roared with laughter. They thought it a huge joke. Careless let them laugh. His quick brain was trying to think of a way out of this situation.

But there aren't many ways of turning the tables on two men leaning their guns into the middle of your back, and Careless wasn't going to indulge in any hasty action that might bring death prematurely.

'Every minute I keep alive gives me a better chance of lickin' 'em,' he thought grimly.

But he was forced to march down that passage, and then they came to the door that gave out on to the waste land behind the saloon. Careless kicked on the door and it flew open.

Outside it was almost dark, but the slanting rays of a dying sun reflected from low hanging clouds and for the moment gave them light.

It wasn't much of a light, but Careless saw—

He saw something whizzing towards him out of the gloom, and instinctively he jerked his head aside. Something slapped against his cheek and then he heard a thud from behind him and a groan, and straightaway a gun clattered on to the board step.

Careless hurled himself sideways, and as he fell he dragged out one of his Colts.

He had a momentary impression of someone leaping up from behind a bush and gliding away on to the mesquite. And that same fleeting impression showed him a man tumbling out through the doorway not a couple of yards from him – a dead man. A man with a tomahawk embedded in his skull.

The second gunman was too startled even to use his gun. At any rate right until that moment O'Connor began to draw that second gunman's finger had not tightened upon the trigger of that ugly Colt.

But the sudden movement of O'Connor brought the gunman whirling round. O'Connor saw the snarl of desperation and fear on the gunman's face. He saw the crouching movement and the quick jerk of the gun as the hammer came back and then began to descend.

Frantically Careless lugged out his gun and in that same movement triggered lead towards his opponent. He got off one round only before his back hit the dust and disturbed his aim. Desperately he rolled, expecting a stream of bullets to find him out in the darkness. But not a shot came.

Instead, Careless heard a sudden scream of pain from the doorway. Lifting his head from the dust, his Colt jerking madly round to take fresh aim on that gunman opponent, Careless was in time to see the figure reel away through the open doorway.

And Careless saw that he was gripping a shoulder that was suddenly discoloured where his hand pressed.

'Winged the maverick,' thought Careless grimly, rolling lithely on to his feet.

The man could be heard stumbling back into the saloon. But there were other sounds now, the sounds of men running from all sides towards the scene of the gunplay.

Careless hesitated for just one second, crouching

there against the shadowy wall of that clapboard building. His eyes raked the shadowy mesquite, seeking for signs of that Indian opponent. But there was no movement on the darkening shrub land.

On an impulse Careless leapt over the body of the tomahawked man and ran into the corridor of the saloon. When he came to his room, he unlocked the door and went inside, locking the door after him. Then he stood in the darkness and waited.

He heard men running up, and listened to their exclamations when they found the dead gunman behind the saloon.

'Tomahawked!'

'Injun work!'

'By gar, there's been Injuns right inside the town!'

Careless grinned to himself in the darkness. He did not want to get involved any deeper into trouble, and without a sheriff in this frontier post there was little he could do if he did go out and explain what had happened.

That thought checked him. What had happened? he wondered.

He shrugged. He had been marched out to meet his death, only it looked as if some Indian had also marked him down and had been waiting out there in the scrub behind the saloon – waiting for him to appear.

That Indian had saved his life, O'Connor realised now. For the whirling tomahawk that had been intended for his skull, instead had killed instantaneously his captor.

'I guess I gotta thank some Injun for that,' O'Connor thought grimly, and wondered which

54

Indian enemy it could be. He guessed it would be one of the Kittewa.

'Mebbe Crazy Elk or one of his hot-headed braves,' he thought. And then he wondered if it had been that medicine man whom he had humbled.

Lying down on his plank bed, he thought that it might be the medicine man. For Careless had shown him up considerably, and a medicine man who loses face is as good as an outcast from his tribe. Maybe that medicine man had been thrown out of the tribe and had been lying out there to exact revenge in consequence.

But O'Connor didn't think long on that subject. He was a very tired man and right then he was determined to get some sleep.

The men at the back of the saloon made a big noise, and by the flash of light through the barred opening that served as a window to his room, he knew they were carrying flaming torches.

He went to sleep all the same, in spite of the noise, and his last thought was that the dead man would have friends among that crowd and he wouldn't know them and they could take a pot at him any time they wanted.

Not a reassuring thought, but big Careless O'Connor fell asleep on it all the same.

Less than one hour later he came leaping out of his bed, as a terrifying scream came through the night air.

That hour's sleep had bemused rather than refreshed him, and for a moment he stood in the darkness by his plank bed, uncertain what to do.

Then he realised that the whole town – this shanty town at the end of the railroad – was in an uproar.

Looking through the window, at first he thought the town was on fire. There was a wild leaping red glow from among the distant buildings where the railroad itself ran. Then he realised that the light must have come from hundreds of flaming torches. A swelling roar came to his ears then. It was the roar of a crowd with a victim, O'Connor knew at once. For he had heard lynching crowds before, and he could recognise that savage, deep-throated roar again.

He didn't want to go out into the town. He wanted to lie there and refresh his weary body, but his instincts as a federal agent impelled him towards the door, nevertheless.

In the dark passage he pulled out each Colt in turn and tested the mechanism. He had a feeling that they were going to be needed now.

He went through the saloon. There wasn't a man in the place save for the proprietor.

O'Connor looked at the fleshy, blue-jowled man, leaning disconsolately on his mopping-up rag, and he said: 'Where's everybody gone to?'

The saloon proprietor made a few unnecessary movements with that filthy rag on the bar top. Then his growling voice said: 'They've got themselves drunk, and now they're aimin' to string up every goldarn Injun in the camp!'

He spat disgustedly into a can of sawdust just over the bar. O'Connor knew that his disgust was not for the unfortunate Indians, but for his loss of trade.

O'Connor started towards the door, and then he

paused. 'You've got nothin' to gripe about!' he said grimly. 'Them fellars must have drunk you dry to get into lynching mood!'

And then, right at the batwings, a thought struck him and again he turned, this time very slowly.

He looked at that blue-chinned man, his eyes full of suspicion. 'You say the whole town got itself fighting drunk – tonight?' There was amazement in his tone.

The proprietor nodded, his expression surly. 'Right good an' tight they all got, here an' in the other saloons.'

O'Connor said: 'Where did they get their money from?' For he knew it wasn't pay-day for another few days, and knowing his Irishers, he knew they hadn't enough money among the lot of them to get one man drunk much less the whole camp.

That was the suspicion in his mind. Very slowly, almost softly, the big Texan asked: 'Who put the drinks up?'

Again that unnecessary movement with the rag. O'Connor caught the flicker of mean eyes on that blue-chinned face. He realised that the saloon proprietor would have preferred not to answer that question, but O'Connor had a fighting reputation and the man thought better of it.

Ungraciously he growled: 'Some guys kept setting 'em up. Some of the gangers. Looks like they've come into a gold-mine, the way they put out the dollars tonight!'

That was all O'Connor wanted to know. His quick brain immediately saw the implication behind his manoeuvre.

As he jumped down the wooden steps on to the dusty roadway, he thought: 'This is the beginning!'

It was a hunch that there was more than a hunch now – that someone was going to stir up big trouble with the local Indians and thus put them back behind schedule again. And he could guess who it was who was behind this trouble.

He started to run between the shadowy buildings to where he could hear the noise of the lynching mob. As he ran he thought of that summons to Washington and his conversation with one of the highest men in the land.

'We have sent for you, O'Connor, because you are our finest frontier agent,' the grey-haired, grey-faced man had said. 'You have been invited here because if any man can help us it is you.'

O'Connor, uneasy in those Washington surroundings, had waited for the statesman to speak more fully.

'As you know, O'Connor, when you become a politician you make enemies.' The man smiled. O'Connor liked that smile. There was a kindness in it. 'And we, because we are in power today in the United States Government, we have earned ourselves our detractors and enemies. There are unscrupulous people whose desire for power is such that they will do everything to discredit us.'

O'Connor was remembering that now as his long legs carried him round the last corner where the torches threw their red reflecting light.

He remembered the story of the unaccountable delays in the railroad construction project which was backed by federal funds down at Santa Fe. 'We are convinced that the delays are deliberately contrived so that our enemies can accuse us of woeful mismanagement of federal funds.'

He was turning that corner then, running into the blaze of light cast by those tossing arches, when again that wild and terrified scream came to his ears. A dread suspicion that was horror leapt into his mind as he guessed something of the identity of that terrified soul.

He came crashing round the corner, forgetting now the mission that had carried him from Washington to Santa Fe, where a lone survivor of an explosives train disaster had given him a clue to the identity of the man bought by Washington politicians.

Joe Butcher – the man who had left that abandoned project to become construction chief of this even more important trans-Continental railroad project in the mid-west of America—

And then Careless saw Joe Butcher. He saw him in the act of riding away from the outskirts of this brawling mob that were centred round a tall telegraph pole.

Careless saw hundreds of drink-crazed men, all with their heads turned towards some centre point.

At first he thought it was the corpses that were dangling from that telegraph pole – the corpses that he knew at once were Indians.

And then he realised that the attraction for the moment was a struggling knot of people on a flat car just behind the telegraph pole.

He saw three huge, scrub-bearded railroad workers, brutal-faced and triumphant. And gripped in their mighty hands was – a girl!

FIVE

'STRING HER UP!'

She was an Indian maiden. Careless saw that in just a fraction of a second as her face became revealed in the light of those waving torches. He saw dark, nearly black desperate eyes that were wide with fear and horror. He saw the long, black, plaited hair that only an Indian could wear.

Then she was lost to sight in her struggles with those three taunting, brutal captors. Careless began to shove his way through the crowd. As he did so he heard one of the men on the flat car, painfully gripping the shrinking girl by the wrist, bellow to the now vast audience: 'I say, string up all Injuns! There's not a one of 'em fit to live in the white man's West!'

An approving roar came up from that unruly crowd at that. Careless saw the flushed faces around him and got the reek of strong liquor on their breath. He knew these men had been deliberately inflamed by drink so that they would be ready to receive any wild and dangerous talk.

'They can't come a-tomahawkin' white men right in the middle of our camp!' that bellowing voice shouted hoarsely; and again there was an approving roar. 'Let's go an' settle with them blamed Kittewa once and for all!'

The speaker had got the mob worked up to the right pitch of excitement. Now they were all with him – now these fighting Irishers were ready to go off on any mad enterprise that promised fun.

But O'Connor was there to try to keep some sort of sanity in that part of the world. This was the very thing he wished to avoid.

As he pushed his way through that throng he was shouting to the men around him: 'Don't listen to that crazy fool! Can't you see it would be death to us all to do as he says?'

They parted to let him go through, and at his words men stared in drunken disbelief at him. 'You skeered of them Kittewas?' someone shouted.

'I ain't skeered!' O'Connor went ploughing on.

'Them few Kittewas is a nuisance. We could wipe 'em out an' not know we've done it!' the speaker shouted after him; and Careless realised that here was one of the paid hirelings of Joe Butcher.

He shouted back for the benefit of the others around him: 'But if you attack the Kittewas, the whole durned Sioux nation will come a-ridin' the war trails, an' we'll be at the end of all them trails!' And then he was right up against the flat car.

He put his big hand on the edge and then looked up. His first glance saw the corpses on that telegraph pole. He recognised one of them. These were the railroad workers. Innocent men had lost their lives to suit the purposes of the cunning Joe Butcher and the men who paid him.

O'Connor filled with anger at the thought and his eyes switched to the girl and her captors. He saw men who were not drunk. Saw men with cunning in their eyes as they regarded him.

O'Connor shouted: 'Take your hands off that gal! Men don't make war with women!'

'She's an Injun.' The speaker, a hulking, unshaven brute who walked with a roll as if he were top-heavy with meat, suddenly came forward and lashed out with his foot, intending to crash his heavy boot into O'Connor's face.

But O'Connor wasn't there. That lazy-looking Westerner could move like greased lightning when he wanted to. At that moment he wanted to.

The boot sailed over O'Connor's shoulder. For one second the surprised railroad ganger stood balanced on the edge of the car, one foot in the air at the end of his kick.

The next, O'Connor had grabbed that extended foot and jerked the man clean off his balance.

There was a roar of dismay and fear as the big, beefy man found himself tossed with incredible ease over O'Connor's head into the midst of the surging crowd.

The crowd roared its delight while at the same time shouting abuse at big Careless O'Connor.

Careless vaulted nimbly on to the flat car. The other two men were still getting over their surprise at what had happened to their comrade. But when they saw Careless coming threateningly towards them, they shouted: 'You keep back! We don't want none of your interference!'

O'Connor braced his legs apart and surveyed them grimly. It was his job as a Federal agent to keep peace with the Indians in the West. He was going to keep peace even if he had to take on the whole thousand men single-handed. Probably those two hulking brutes with the Indian girl between them recognised that.

One went for his gun. O'Connor started to go for his gun, too, but then he realised that the girl would be thrown forward as a shield and would receive his bullets. He saw that desperate imploring brown face and went diving suddenly down at their feet.

A roar filled the night air almost in his ear. He was deafened, and he got the acrid odour of gunpowder fumes in his nostrils as he rolled.

Then his heavy body rolled among legs, his arms whirled round and gripped behind those legs. Three people went tumbling headfirst over him on to the box car.

He heard grunted shouts of dismay from the two hucksters, and a sudden high-pitched cry of alarm from the girl.

He couldn't help it if the girl tumbled with the men. At least it made the men release their grip on her.

O'Connor was up first. The girl was on her knees. O'Connor took her by the shoulders and in one swift movement had lifted her to her feet and thrust her behind him. Then he dived into his opponents.

They were coming round quickly, snarling and going for their guns. O'Connor kicked a gun out of a hand that was jerking back a hammer. It exploded in mid-air as he kicked it over the heads of the crowd.

Then the three of them were fighting like Kilkenny cats, at too close quarters to be able to use their guns.

It was a weird scene, with that roaring, exulting crowd holding their red-burning torches to light the scene. Three men fought as if in a boxing-ring, elevated there on top of that flat car that had brought rails in.

O'Connor realised that he was up against two tough fighters, men who knew all the tricks including the dirty ones. These men owed their positions as gangers to their ability to subdue even the most truculent of the Irish labourers who worked under them.

They came crowding him, one of them stamping to break the bones in his feet, another leaping in with knees kicking to get into his stomach.

O'Connor took some of the punishment, though he got his feet out of the way of those stamping hobnailed boots. Then he went in as if their blows had no effect on his mighty frame.

He went in with his fists digging like pistons into his opponents' bodies.

There was a flurry of wild and savage fighting with boots flying and fists hacking. And the crowd was going crazy in their appreciation of a good fight.

Then Careless O'Connor got his fist travelling from somewhere around waist level, and it crashed into one unshaven face and that was the end of that opponent. He went toppling off the edge of the flat car.

O'Connor was left with one opponent. He went in coldly and mercilessly, without sympathy for this man who was prepared to hang innocent Indians in his effort to foment trouble.

The man knew he was in for a thrashing, and a streak of yellow showed. He started to run backwards round the flat car, trying to protect himself and find a place where he might jump off.

Contemptuously O'Connor jumped in, his mighty hands reaching out and gripping that big, plug-ugly by the neck of his dirty shirt.

O'Connor dragged him round to face the crowd. Then he shouted: 'This man is paid to make trouble with you. He and his pards want to develop this Injun war so that the railroad project will be stopped an' politicians in Washington make capital of it. Don't listen to him! Don't go ridin' into Kittewa country—'

Suddenly, within the crowd, men began to shout and drowned his voice. The hirelings of Joe Butcher were suddenly alarmed at the prospect of their plans being upset by one man, this big, lean Texan.

Now a mob of men came thrusting their way through a crowd which wasn't sure which way to turn now. There were plenty of them, a dozen or so. O'Connor saw one of them with his shoulder bandaged, and recognised him for his opponent earlier that evening.

He tried to shout the truth down to the crowd, but now no one was listening to him.

O'Connor saw that mob of evil-eyed men fighting

to get to the flat car, and he realised that he was in a bad position.

He looked round. Which ever way he looked that flat car was surrounded and men were converging on him from all sides.

He felt someone grip his arm timidly. He looked down. The Indian girl was terrified, and had come close to him as if seeking protection.

O'Connor's face was grim. There wasn't much he could do if a dozen or more vicious merciless brutes stormed that flat car. He might decorate that telegraph-pole along with the Indians, he thought.

But in Kittewa he said to the girl: 'You stay by my side. I won't go under without a fight, and I'll do all I can to protect you.'

She nodded, understanding his words. And then, as O'Connor started to look away from her, a thought struck him and his eyes swept back to that lovely young Indian face.

'Gal, I've seen you before!'

She nodded. Suddenly he realised who it was.

'You tried to stand in my way at the Kittewa camp last night.'

She whispered: 'I am Gentle Fawn.'

But before he could ask any more questions, before he could think to ask why she was here in a white man's town, he had to turn his attention to where men were trying to clamber on to the car.

He jumped across and lashed out, and a man went toppling into the crowd.

Then men were on to the flat car behind him, and suddenly there were half-a-dozen of them driving for him with fists and boots lashing out to maim and hurt him. Too late he decided to go for his guns.

For a few seconds big Careless seemed to live in a world of pain. Boots hacked cruelly at his legs. Fists that were like steel-hard pile-drivers tore through his defences and smashed into his face.

There was frenzied fighting for a few moments, for Careless hit back and hurt. But it was hopeless. They were swarming all over him, big, unshaven huskies, with malice in their eyes and no pity in their hearts.

Careless heard a cry of terror from that Indian girl again, and he saw her being lifted by some of the laughing brutes, and they started to take her away.

Somehow he found the strength to fight his way to her side, sending her captors flying because of the ferocity and unexpectedness of his attack. His arms went around the girl and pulled her back, and then the whole mob in fury turned on him and girl and man went down on to the rough boards of the flat car.

Now it was all over. The boots were kicking in, and there was no chance of escape for the pair. A boot crashed on to Careless' unprotected head and his senses swam.

And then all those brutal adversaries came toppling down on their faces alongside Careless, and the blows ceased.

Dimly Careless realised that the flat car had been dealt a mighty shock, as if something had run into it. Now Careless realised that they were moving, and heard the cries of alarm as the crowd tried to get off the track ahead of the moving flat car.

He struggled on to his elbows, the blood streaming from his cut face. The Indian girl was crouching against him, her eyes wide with terror, as if still looking to Careless to give her protection.

Careless saw figures nimbly leap on to the moving flat car. He thought bitterly, dully: 'More of 'em!'

Then he saw one broad-shouldered track man seize a fallen huckster and sling him on to the track.

The other newcomers tore into those fallen bullies and pitched them back to their fellows among the crowd. Careless struggled to his feet.

He saw a familiar face – Tom Riordan's.

Old Tom came grinning up to him, rubbing his hands together as if he had enjoyed smacking someone whom he didn't like. He braced his legs apart to balance on that moving truck and called above the roar of the infuriated crowd: 'We got here just in time, Careless!'

Careless' face, stiff from the blows it had received, cracked open in a grin of relief. 'I sure guess you did, pardner.'

The Indian girl didn't trust the other white men, and she was standing close against Careless now. He put his arm about her slim shoulders to hold her erect while he looked round.

Behind them a small, shunting train had driven a line of trucks on to the flat car and was steadily trundling out towards the end of the line. All around them men were running to keep pace with the flat car, a horde of infuriated, drunk-maddened men whose faces shone redly under those waving torches.

They did not like this interruption to their sport. They had been inflamed against these Indians, and

Careless's intervention had turned their fury against him.

Now they wanted to lynch them both, the man and the girl.

The little group of Riordan's supporters sat with their legs over the edge of the flat car and jeered at the men who were losing the race to keep up with the train. The angrier the mob grew, the more cheerfully insulting were the replies thrown back by Riordan's little force. In their midst stood Careless and the Indian girl, recovering from their recent ordeal. Gradually they saw the mob fall behind, though some of them tried to board the engine but were beaten off by Riordan's men posted on the foot plate.

Then Riordan turned towards Careless. They could only just see his face now because they were moving into the darkness.

Riordan said abruptly, 'We can't go much further, Careless. Half-a-mile and we'll be right at the end of the track, then them varmints will catch up with us.'

Careless could see the dim shapes of the last of the huts of the little railroad township. He said quickly, 'Guess this is where we get off, then. I reckon I'll find some place to hide away until morning.'

With morning, he'd be able to hold his own with his guns against any mob, he thought grimly. He realised also that by morning most of this crowd would have got over this anger with him when they were sober.

Riordan nodded. 'Get off quickly,' he said. 'We'll come with you.'

Careless swung over the edge of the flat car. The

other men were already dropping off and rolling into the sand along the edge of the track.

Careless put one foot on the grease box that covered the end of the axle. He looked up at the Indian girl. He did not speak, but clinging with one hand, held out the other towards her.

Trustingly she sat over the edge of the car. Careless put his arm round her slim waist, stood erect, holding her out over the edge of the track, and then he jumped wide, his long legs taking the shock immediately he hit the loose sand.

For a second he staggered under the force of that landing, his legs trying to break the fall. Then he tripped and both rolled over, but neither suffered and they sat up on the warm earth.

They didn't stay long there. Behind them raged the mob, their torches dancing as they approached less than a couple of hundred yards away. Then Careless heard the thunder of hooves and knew that some of the mob had found horses.

He jumped to his feet, pulling the girl up beside him. The train was rattling by now, with Riordan standing by the track shouting instructions to the passing engine driver. The rest of Riordan's men had already disappeared into the darkness. If they were caught by the mob their lives wouldn't be worth anything, O'Connor knew.

Neither would his, he remembered, and he plunged away into the darkness, dragging the Indian girl by her hand.

In a few moments, though, the girl was keeping pace easily with him. O'Connor was handicapped by the high heels of his riding boots, and the girl was as fleet-footed as the fawn from which she was named.

They circled and came back among the sprawling buildings which were thrown without any apparent system or order on the hard-baked ground. Careless knew where he was going.

He ran round to where a swinging lamp revealed the wide door to the livery stable where his horse was kept. He went inside stealthily, but the place was deserted. Apparently the owner of the livery stable was out on the track, too.

O'Connor looked at his horse which turned at the familiar scent of its master. It would be easy to mount and ride away into the desert, he knew, but he didn't want to run away from trouble. He decided that he might just as well sleep in comfort inside this town as out on the desert.

There was a ladder which led to a hayloft above the stables, and now Careless motioned towards it and the girl glided forward in the lamplight and went up the steps with the lithe ease and grace which was habitual with Indians. O'Connor followed.

The girl was standing on the edge of the trap door, uneasy at the darkness around her. O'Connor struck a match. There was plenty of hay in big bales around the edge of the trap door, and while the match lasted he kicked one open and spread the contents at his feet. Carefully extinguishing the match, he whispered to the girl. 'Here's where we stay tonight, gal. Make yourself comfortable.'

In the darkness he lay down in the hay, stretching gratefully in the sweet-smelling fodder. All he wanted now was to catch up on the sleep he had missed in the past couple of nights.

He heard the girl carefully lower herself into the hay and curl round. He was so sore that he didn't want to speak. His face was now like a stiffened mask and it throbbed and was painful.

All the same, there were things he wanted to know.

'Tell me more about your comin' to this town.'

She told him. She trusted this big white man, though she trusted no other paleface. Her mate to be, White Knife, had disappeared from the camp. She had guessed that he had come in search of Careless, in an attempt to re-establish his lost dignity.

O'Connor grinned in the darkness. 'You mean, he thought that if he got my scalp he'd be a big fellar with the boys back in your Kittewa camp?'

That was it. O'Connor's hair meant a lot to a fierce young Indian warrior.

She had come to the town to seek for him, to tell White Knife of things that had happened in his absence. And drunken white men had caught her in the town.

The most important event, she explained to O'Connor, was that the medicine man had been thrown out of the tribe. That interested O'Connor and he stirred in the hay and whispered across the darkness questions to the girl.

She answered them. O'Connor's magic had been so much better than the medicine man's that now the tribe would not take the medicine man seriously. And immediately the chiefs had declared against the medicine man, interesting things began to emerge.

'Such as?'

One young brave had reported that he had more than once seen the medicine man in conversation with a mysterious paleface who rode out from the railroad camp. The tribe, realising that their medicine man had thus been having truck with the hated paleface, were incensed and would have torn their medicine man limb from limb, only when they came to look for him he had disappeared from their midst.

'What was the paleface like?' Careless wanted to know.

The girl described him, whispering in the Kittewa tongue. She could only say she had heard the young brave tell the elders of the tribe.

But as she spoke, a picture began to form in Careless's mind. A big, heavy man. A man not so young, with a red face and heavy moustache. A man with plenty of meat on his shoulders.

That could be a description of Joe Butcher.

Careless was thinking grimly in that darkness. 'Looks like Joe Butcher and that crooked medicine man have been cooking plots.'

Butcher would be using the cunning medicine man to keep up the attacks by the tribe which had been putting the railroad construction job behind schedule.

The one consoling feature was that quite inadvertently Careless had upset the scheme. Apparently his own 'magic' had caused the medicine man to be thrown out of the tribe – he had to grin at the thought of that magic. Lip reading and a trick knife had done it!

But he had not long for satisfaction. As he lay back on the hay, thinking and dozing on again, he became suddenly wide awake and alert.

There had been a stealthy movement down below in the stable and to Careless's practised ears he knew it was no horse.

The girl's quick ears had caught the sound, too, and suddenly she was terrified again. Careless felt her wriggle closer to him and he could even hear the thumping of her heart in that stillness. Her hand sought his and then they lay there and waited.

Whoever it was, was coming to the ladder that led up to the loft. And whoever it was, was proceeding with the utmost caution.

They heard a creak as weight was put on to a rung of that ladder and they knew that the intruder was ascending towards them.

Careless put his hand on his Colt. He did not want to use it, because that would bring unwelcome attention upon them. Yet if danger pressed, he would.

It seemed an age before they heard a further sound. This newcomer was moving as if in deadly dread of being detected. Slowly, rung by rung, he came towards the manhole. Just at that moment a new sound obtruded. It was the sound of a mob approaching the stable.

Evidently the mob had chased the train to the end of the track, only to find it deserted. Now they were marching back towards the town, doubtless intent on finding the authors of their discomfiture.

The sound must have disturbed this intruder. Just when Careless was expecting to see the head and shoulders revealed against the faint reflected light from the lamp, they heard a soft thud as if the stranger had changed his mind and descended to the ground again.

There was a swift patter of feet and they knew that he had gone outside. Whoever it was did not want to be trapped inside the building when the mob reached the town, Careless thought.

Perhaps, the thought occurred to him, the mob had saved him a piece of unpleasantness, then, only he didn't feel grateful to that lynching party!

The girl withdrew, now that the danger had passed. Perhaps she had become shy, as an Indian maiden would, and Careless felt her hand pull away slowly from his. He lay back again. His other hand was no longer on the butt of his Colt. Now he tried to keep awake because that mob was obviously searching the town, and that meant that they might come into this building.

Careless hadn't expected a building-by-building search. But all to quickly they heard the stampings and the shoutings of the drunken railroad workers. The light grew up in the loft as men with torches came along the front of the livery stable. Hoarse voices called to each other: 'You take that building. We'll take this. Search it from floor to roof. If them pesky critters is hidin' in this town by golly we're gonna find 'em!'

Now Careless wished that he had taken to horse and ridden far away from the town! The girl was back close against him now, terrified at once more falling into the hands of these brutal palefaces.

Careless put his arm protectingly about her. They wouldn't get this girl from him while he lived, he thought. And now the Colt was out of its holster and resting on his muscular thigh.

The stamping of feet grew louder. Men had actually entered the livery stable. Up above the restless horses the big Texan and the Indian maiden froze into absolute stillness, there among that sweet-smelling hay. Both felt that the slightest movement, the smallest sound, would attract attention on them.

They heard voices. Men were crowding into the doorway below, and the dancing torch light was frightening the horses and they were beginning to kick.

Someone shouted in coarse, harsh tones, 'This stable's a likely place for 'em. Come on, boys, let's go right through the place.'

O'Connor's hand tightened upon his Colt butt. It was coming! he thought, and he racked his brains desperately to think of some way of saving this Indian maiden from them. He decided he would hide her in the hay and drop down and fight it out with his opponents.

Men were crowding towards the foot of the ladder. There was a tremendous noise, as whinnying horses added to the babble of sound.

Then, just as they heard those ladder rungs creak again, a stentorian voice bellowed. 'You come outa there!'

O'Connor recognised the voice. Joe Butcher's!

There was a momentary silence below as the boss ganger's voice was recognised by the other railroad men.

Then a man said hoarsely, 'We're lookin' for them pair that got away, boss. We figger up in the hay loft's as good a place as any for them to hide. We're gonna find 'em if we have to search every inch of this town!'

Joe Butcher's loud voice suddenly silenced the speaker. 'You wont' find 'em in this building,' he said confidently. 'There's been someone here all the time. You're wasting your time. Better git out around the town an' look for 'em somewhere else.'

Gentle Fawn did not understand the harsh words of Joe Butcher, but O'Connor did and he lay in the way and listened with amazement. Joe Butcher was saying they could not possibly be inside this building because it had been watched all the time!

If it had been watched all the time then Joe Butcher must know they were inside the livery stable!

The boss ganger's words had their effect on the men. They were anxious to find the missing pair, and if Joe Butcher said they were wasting their time they didn't propose to remain in the livery stable any longer.

Up above, Careless and Gentle Fawn heard the men stamp out and go streaming across to search another building. For a few moments they thought they were alone in the livery stable, and then they heard Joe Butcher speak again and it was evident that a few of the men still remained.

'They nearly found that durned Injun,' Joe Butcher said harshly. 'We came just in time to prevent 'em going up them steps!'

They heard heavy footsteps and then a creak as if someone had leaned against the ladder. And then

Joe Butcher called softly, 'You c'n come down now. They've all gone.'

Nothing happened. So Joe Butcher called again impatiently. 'Come on down you blamed Kittewa Injun. I tell you you've got nothin' to fear. They're all friends down here and we need you.'

Again there was no movement from the left as O'Connor and Gentle Fawn lay rigidly silent together in that warm soft hay. Below they heard Joe Butcher's surprised voice.

'Looks like the blamed Injun ain't there at all. I told him to hide up there until I was ready for him. Here, Ben, you go up an' see if he's hidin' there. Mebbe he don't trust my word that we're all friends down here.'

This was it! O'Connor heard the creak of those rungs yet again. Someone mounted the ladder. They saw a hat brim shoved back, and the outline of a man's face against the light from below.

The man halted, resting his elbows on the edge of the trap door and peering all around him. Then, to O'Connor's dismay and horror of that Indian maiden, they saw the man fumble in his vest pocket for a match.

Now they would be seen.

Now, thought O'Connor grimly, there was going to be gun play!

SIX

'THE MASSACRE.'

Just at which moment there was an exclamation from some other man in the stable below.

'Hey, Joe, here's your Injun!'

Below they heard the sound of men turning. Then Joe Butcher's sharp voice said, 'I thought I told you to keep out of the way in the hay loft? You know you might run into trouble in this town walkin' around tonight.'

There was a murmur as a new voice made some explanation. Both Gentle Fawn and O'Connor recognised that voice.

It was the Kittewa medicine man's!

Ben, the man on the ladder, shoved back his matches and descended. Both the Indian maiden and the big Texan released their breath in a sigh of tremendous relief. Yet again had danger been averted!

O'Connor realised what had happened. That

mysterious intruder earlier had been the medicine man, coming to hide in this very hay loft on the instructions of Joe Butcher. But, Indian like, he hadn't liked the darkness and the sense of confinement that comes within the white man's buildings. He had instead stolen out and hidden elsewhere, even though that put him in danger of the many search parties of white men looking for O'Connor and the Indian maiden.

O'Connor switched his thoughts back to the men below. They had all the air of conspirators gathering for some desperate enterprise.

Joe Butcher did most of the talking, and his voice was low and guarded, as if he knew he was committing himself by his speech and didn't intend unwelcome ears to know what he was up to. But clearly he was with like spirits for he spoke openly, frankly of what he was plotting.

'We've got them men well and truly het up agen the blamed Injuns. That bit of tomahawkin' right here in the camp sure has got the men riled.'

Joe Butcher chuckled hoarsely, as if tickled at the way events had played right into his hands.

'An' bein' bested by that nosey-parker of a Federal agent an' the Injun gal hasn't made their tempers any sweeter. Them galoots is just as we want 'em. They'll do as we tell 'em now.'

There was a pause, and O'Connor knew that below Joe Butcher was listening and Careless wondered if he had made any slight sound. Now he hardly dared to breathe for fear of giving away their hiding-place. They would not live long if Joe Butcher knew they were overhearing his desperate plans.

Then, to their relief, Joe went on, 'We're gonna hit that Kittewa village afore dawn. You hear me, you men? You're goin' out right now to raise as big a posses as you can, an' we're gonna meet down by the sidin' ready to hit the trail. Bring guns – rifles if they've got 'em – an' enough food an' water to last 'em till tomorrow afternoon.'

Another voice interrupted. 'You think we c'n find the Injuns in that short time, shoot 'em up, an' then get back to camp? All in around twelve or fifteen hours?'

Joe Butcher said complacently, 'I sure do. That's why we've got Black Eye here, the Kittewa medicine man.' His voice rumbled with cynical laughter. 'He's kinda sore agen his tribe, this medicine man. The tribe thought his medicine wasn't much good compared with O'Connor's an' they slung the critter out of camp.

'He'll ride with us tonight an' show us where his people are. I reckon this fellar sure is a bad hater. I wouldn't like him to be agen me!'

Gentle Fawn hadn't understood this, and Careless risked whispering a translation into Kittewa for her benefit. He felt the grip on his arm grow until it almost hurt him. Gentle Fawn was incensed at the traitorous conduct of this man who had once led the tribe.

O'Connor's grip over her hand cautioned her to make no betraying sound or movement, though he was just as incensed against the rascally medicine man as the girl.

81

Joe Butcher's voice was brisk now. 'You've got your instructions. Go get them men rounded up immediately. Don't bring any soft-hearted critters along with you. I want tough men for this night's work. Be ready in quarter of an hour to hit the trail. I'm takin' the Injun along with me!'

There was a flurry of activity below, as the men ran out into the night, shouting instructions. They heard Joe Butcher and others saddling up horses, and then, five minutes later, the place was silent again as the little group rode out from the livery stable towards the railway yards.

Immediately their enemies had disappeared, O'Connor rolled stiffly on to his knees. He was still very bruised and sore from that manhandling he had received, but the urgency of the night's work before him made him ignore his sufferings. He pulled the girl towards the edge of the trapdoor.

'You've got to go with me tonight, sweetheart,' he said. 'I can't leave you on your own in this man's town, I reckon!'

Cautiously he descended the ladder, peering into the gloom of the stables. To his relief he saw that his horse had not been taken by the men who had ridden out with Joe Butcher. That had been a fear on his mind.

He assisted Gentle Fawn to descend the ladder softly, and then, when they were on firm ground again, he immediately ran across and saddled up his horse. He put a saddle and bridle on a smaller black horse which looked to have speed and mounted the Indian maiden on it. Leading the two horses outside, he sprang into his saddle, holding on to the bridle rein of the Indian girl's so that they would not become separated in the dark.

Outside was a confusion of gloom and shadows, because few lamps burned in any of the huts, and the men with the torches had by now all moved to the north end of the town. They could hear their voices in the distance and guessed that Joe Butcher's men were already recruiting desperadoes for the ride into Kittewa territory.

Careless rode straight for the shack in which lived Tom Riordan and some other workers. But when he got there Riordan was absent.

No doubt Riordan was keeping out of the way until the drunken mob had forgotten the part he had played in rescuing O'Connor and Gentle Fawn from their grasp.

Perplexed, O'Connor drew rein and peered around into the darkness. It was unlikely he would be able to find Riordan or any of his friends until daylight, and the only people he might encounter in the town now were enemies.

While he was hesitating there, pondering on his next action, he heard the thunder of hoofs as a cavalcade swept out of the town to the north of him.

'Darn it!' he muttered to himself, 'There goes Joe Butcher an' his Injun fighters!'

That settled things for O'Connor. There was no way of stopping that mob from riding into Kittewa territory, but there was just a possibility that he, O'Connor, guided by the girl, might somehow get ahead of the hucksters and give the tribe warning.

O'Connor didn't think of the risks he was taking. He knew the appalling consequences if the liquor-crazy mob got through and shot up that Kittewa village.

The Sioux nation would not countenance such a hostile act against their own brethren, even the despised and detested Kittewas. For certain they would don their war bonnets, paint themselves for the war trail, and come thundering down from the hills in a ride of vengeance.

O'Connor had visions of a land at war for months on end – of this railroad destroyed perhaps for even a hundred miles back eastwards. And while men were fighting they could not be building, and the railroad project would be at a standstill.

That would please the political enemies of the present government.

So O'Connor set off into the night, leading Gentle Fawn on her black mare, intent on beating the hucksters to their victims. He rode west for a while and then struck off southward. He knew his way in the approximate direction of the Kittewas camp.

It was true he had found them the previous day, but it was likely that the Kittewas had moved since then and he might have to spend hours in searching for them.

If it had been light he would have tried to trail the Butcher men, but that was too hazardous in the dark. He could not afford to run into the gang. So he had to take a chance on finding his way past them in the dark until he came to Kittewa country. Then Gentle Fawn would no doubt be able to lead him to the camp.

All night they rode, slumping wearily in their saddles as the hours took the strength from them. When dawn came they halted where a spring bubbled in an arroyo. O'Connor dismounted and helped the girl out of her saddle.

They both went down on their faces and drank, and then sat back and ate some buffalo meat that was in O'Connor's saddle-bag. The horses waded into the water and drank noisily, and then came wearily out and stood with heads hanging, too tired to forage for grass. But there was still some distance ahead for them to go.

O'Connor looked around and got his bearings. He was inside Kittewa country now, and it was time that Gentle Fawn took over. He spoke to her.

'Gentle Fawn, I want you to lead the way now. I want to go to your tribe and tell them that enemies are about to descend upon them.'

This was the first explanation he had given to the girl of their night journey. Perhaps she had thought they were just riding away from their enemies in the town, though she had known of the expedition that had ridden out to attack her people.

Her eyes widened. She protested in Kittewa, her face fearful. 'My people, they will kill you if they see you. They do not like you, even though you came and tried to help them.'

O'Connor slowly got to his feet. The sun's rays were beginning to warm him and he watched the mists chase away, as the heat dried off the night dew. He thought he saw a movement back along the trail and kept his eyes fixed on that spot while he spoke.

'Mebbe. But I've got to ride on just the same, Gentle Fawn. I figger I c'n take care of myself, an' I just can't stand by an' let them murderin' hucksters ride in an' destroy your village. That would mean another war with the Sioux nation.'

Once again he ordered her to mount and lead the way. No movement had come back along the trail. He decided it was a trick of his eyes caused by these swiftly dissolving morning mists, and he turned away his head.

Gentle Fawn stood before him, her head bowed meekly, but not, it turned out, submissively.

He heard her voice whisper: 'That I cannot do, O White Man. I am yours, but I cannot lead you to your death because of my great love for you.'

It was a few seconds before Gentle Fawn's words sank in. O'Connor had been in the act of pushing back that disgraceful, sweat-rimmed hat of his, but at her words his hand paused irresolute. Then his eyes switched round to look at the girl.

'What's this you're sayin'?' he exploded. Gentle Fawn stood there beside him, her eyes downcast, an attractive flush on that smooth brown cheek of hers.

'Goldurn it,' whispered Careless to himself. 'So that's your mind.'

Because he had rescued the girl, looked after her, and now had brought her with him away from the white man's town, she was getting ideas into her pretty head.

She had thought that he was taking her as his mate, and evidently she was liking the idea!

'Glory be!' O'Connor exclaimed, aghast. He could

hold his own against gunmen with flaming six-shoot-ers, but he was considerably out of his depth with this Indian maiden.

His hand continued towards his hat, and he scratched his head in perplexity. He liked this girl and did not want to hurt her feelings, but there was no room in his life for an Indian maiden.

He tried to explain this: 'Gentle Fawn, I am look-ing after you like a father!' He made his tone very stern and elderly.

Her eyes fluttered towards his. 'I do not want you for a father,' she said softly.

O'Connor gulped. He tried a new tack. 'Look here, Gentle Fawn, you're due to take White Knife for your mate!'

'White Knife!' Those lovely flashing eyes leapt towards his and they were brimming with scorn. 'White Knife he is a boy. You are a man!' Her eyes dropped demurely. 'I want a man for mate, not a boy who is defeated in battle!'

O'Connor began to take a grip on himself. He licked his lips, pulled his hat down hard over his head, and said: 'You get many more ideas like that into your pretty head an' I'll tan you where your mother should've tanned you!'

Gentle Fawn didn't understand his words, because he had relapsed into English. But his meaning was clear.

She pouted, stepping away from him, and her eyes brimmed with tears. Suddenly she turned and went running away up the arroyo, as fleet as a young deer.

O'Connor called, 'Come back.' But she ran on.

He knew he could not catch her on that rough ground in his high-heeled riding boots, so he leapt on to his horse and urged it into a gallop. He caught up with her and swept her up from the ground in his mighty arms. Then he halted his horse and spoke sternly to her while she sat across the horse's neck before him.

She was weeping softly, and such a display of emotion was unusual for an Indian. But then she had thought that this mighty white man did want her, and she had been proud of it. Never had she thought to have such a man for a mate! To find that her hopes were unfounded filled her with despair and shame. Now she would not look up at the big Texan.

He spoke to her. 'Lookit here, Gentle Fawn. These things don't work out, see? I've got a job to do here, then my Government will send me mebbe half the length of America away. There ain't no place in my life for gals.'

He tried to soften the blow. Patted her hand clumsily. 'I reckon you're a fine gal, an' I couldn't do better than pick you as my mate.'

He looked at her again. She was as lovely as any creature he had ever seen before. For a moment he wondered if in fact he was right in saying there could be no girl in his life. For a moment he could think of a life with this graceful, beautiful Indian girl.

Then he remembered his job – that work which carried him from one scene of fighting to another. There certainly was no room for any girl, Indian or white, in his fighting life!

Having made up his mind, now he suddenly found

he could handle the situation. He made a joke of it, in a way.

As he turned his horse to ride back, he put his arms around her and gave her a good-natured hug. 'Just for one moment I began to think I should change my mind,' he said, picking his words carefully in the Kittewa tongue. 'Believe me, O Gentle Fawn, there is no girl I have ever met whom I would prefer to your lovely charms!'

The way he handled it helped, but there was an uneasy feeling in the back of O'Connor's mind that the girl was not accepting the situation as he wanted her to. But then she was primitive, wild, half-savage, and these creatures did not behave like the settlers' daughters back east. These Indian maidens were fighters like their menfolk, and he had a feeling that there was going to be trouble because he had turned down this Indian maiden.

When he was back in the arroyo, he reined in his horse abruptly. Something had happened in those few minutes that his back was turned.

The other horse had gone!

O'Connor's first action was to jerk his rifle out of its scabbard. He pulled back the safety catch, holding the gun like a pistol against his side. His eyes leapt from cover to cover, seeking that horse – and the possible enemy. For he knew the horse would not voluntarily have left that water in its tired condition. Someone, he knew, had stolen away with it.

Nothing moved. The sun was beating fully upon them now, throwing long shadows. On either side rocks reared above this belt of green vegetation that grew where the water ran.

His eyes looked down into the dusty ground for sign.

He saw where their two horses had come straight up to the spring. He saw a single set of hoof marks go back along those tracks and then branch leftwards, heading south. Lifting his eyes, he followed those tracks where they went out of sight beyond the end of the arroyo.

He felt he was safe, but all the same he descended carefully, crouching beside his horse and holding his gun at the alert. Gentle Fawn, alarmed, slipped down and stood behind him. She whispered, 'Have our enemies found us?' Squinting against the bright rays of the early morning sun, O'Connor shook his head. He walked forward a few yards and the girl came close behind him. A slight indentation on the sandy soil attracted his attention. Looking carefully around, he went down on one knee and gave a swift examination of that mark.

He pointed. 'Moccasin?' Gentle Fawn looked at the footmark and nodded.

An Indian had stolen their horse away. O'Connor remembered that momentary impression he'd had of someone lurking on the trail behind him. Now he cursed himself for not taking greater precautions. There had been someone behind those rocks all the time, only waiting for a moment when his back would be turned so that the Indian could steal one of their precious horses.

And Gentle Fawn's flight up the valley had given the Indian just such an opportunity.

O'Connor couldn't blame the girl, so he blamed himself instead. But now this made a very unpleasant situation for them. It meant that the pair would have to ride two up, and his horse was tired and wouldn't last long bearing a double burden. O'Connor had a feeling that they were probably ahead of the Butcher gang, but any lead they had would soon be lost if they had to compete on a heavily-burdened horse.

'The Butcher's going to get through,' Careless told himself. 'There's nothin' to stop him winning that race now!'

All the same, he was going to try to beat the gang. He went back to his horse, watching over his shoulder all the while. There was no danger, however, and he mounted and then pulled up the girl beside him.

They walked on to the desert, following the footprints of the stolen horse. When they came round the corner they could see the thief in the far distance. At least they saw a tiny speck that was horse and rider gradually disappearing into the foothills.

It was impossible to recognise the figure, or even to see it was an Indian, because of the distortion caused by the waves of heat that now came shimmering up from the hot desert before them. But O'Connor was sure it was that thieving Indian.

There was nothing he could do about it, the man being beyond range of a rifle. In less than a quarter of an hour the Indian and that horse were completely beyond sight. Careless and Gentle Fawn followed at a slower pace into the hills.

Most of the morning they climbed on foot, to rest the horse on the steeper slopes. And the way Gentle

Fawn directed, they were going right into the mountains. Truly, the Kittewa had moved their camp from the night before. Probably they were afraid that if one white man could find them, then so could others. And they were taking no risks.

They did not come across the tracks of the Butcher gang, but that was not remarkable as the other mob could have entered these mountains by any of a dozen passes paralleling their own.

At noon, when the sun was highest and hottest, they sank down together in the shade of the pines that clothed this mountain side hereabouts. Looking back, they could see right across the land they had traversed, almost as far as the railroad itself. But ahead of them were only rolling, pine-clad hills, and no other human being was in sight.

They rested awhile, and then wearily took up the trail again, O'Connor leading the horse and dragging tired Gentle Fawn by the hand. They had gone perhaps twenty paces when in the far distance came a solitary crack of a rifle.

They halted, aghast. Then a ragged fusillade rang out. The firing continued intermittently for a few minutes, and then became less frequent until finally there was silence.

O'Connor looked at the girl and then held out his hand helplessly. He shook his head. 'I reckon them varmints got to your people ahead of us, Gentle Fawn. I reckon by now they've pretty well shot up your village.'

And he thought, 'That treacherous medicine man ought to have his blamed neck broken for leadin' white men against his own people!' That was a thing O'Connor could not approve of. He was often at war with the Indians, but he did not go for traitors.

They went on, even so, and two hours later came upon the scene of the massacre. The village had been burnt, and they looked upon charred buffalo hides that had dropped when the flames had eaten through the supporting posts of the tipis. And they saw Kittewa people in their last agonies all around them.

It was not a pleasant sight, but that Indian maiden, used to scenes of barbarism, did not show any great distress. Instead, she stood by the horse while the big white man tramped around that village, seeking for signs of life among the bodies that were strewn everywhere.

But Joe Butcher's mob had been thorough. Not an Indian remained alive.

When Careless was sure of this he stood up, his face set and grim, and looked about him.

The heat was oppressive now, with the sun blazing fully upon him in that opening. Around him were the pine trees and the thick bushes that grew close around the glade in which the Indians had made their camp. It was very high in the mountains, and Careless realised that it would be cold at night and decided it was better if they made tracks. But as he stood there he had an uneasy feeling that all was not well. It was the kind of feeling he had sometimes received when he was being watched.

Covertly big Careless O'Connor watched the hemming bushes around him. Suddenly they began to look sinister. Behind them could hide a horde of Indians – maybe some survivors!

He began to walk around a neck of bushes that cut him off from a view of Gentle Fawn and his horse. His hand gripped his rifle and the safety catch was off. Suddenly he was certain that someone was watching him and he was alert and ready for danger.

He told himself: 'Gentle Fawn's watching. She'll sing out soon enough if she sees danger!' And an Indian girl's eyes were sharp and he would get ample warning.

It was with that thought in his mind that he came to an abrupt stop. For a thought also came to him! Would Gentle Fawn warn him of danger?

He remembered that he had turned down her overtures of love back along the trail, and she was fiercely primitive, and these Indian maidens could hate as easily as love. Perhaps, he thought suddenly, that girl would not warn him if danger struck out at him. Perhaps she would think it evened scores because he had turned her down!

And then the thought came to him that perhaps she might have betrayed him another way. Perhaps she might have ridden off on his horse, leaving him stranded high up in these hostile mountains! After all, that was what the other Indian had done back at the arroyo. He had stolen a valuable horse and it might have put an idea into Gentle Fawn's brooding mind.

The thought alarmed him. Impulsively he crashed through that neck of bushes, intent only on breaking through without loss of time to where he had left Gentle Fawn with the horse.

The bushes parted. Ahead of him he saw – nothing. His horse and Gentle Fawn had gone!

The shock of the betrayal brought him to a standstill again, just on the edge of the bushes. A seething anger rose in him and he shook the rifle in his mighty hands to think how easily he had let himself be duped like this. A movement came behind him. He whirled. Too late. A war club crashed against the side of his head.

Careless pulled his head frantically on one side to avert the descending blow, and that saved his life. As it was, it hit him a glancing blow, and yet there was such tremendous power behind it that he was felled like a log, paralysed for the moment by the effect of that stunning, treacherous blow.

Yet in some curious way, though for seconds he had no power to move his limbs, his eyes remained open and he could see and in a vague way understand.

He saw a man leaning out from behind the bushes, his face distorted with the fury that must accompany a killing. An Indian's face.

White Knife's!

There was murder on White Knife's face. For not only had this big white man humbled him and caused him to leave his tribe, but he had seen Oak-O-Nur with his arms about the Indian maiden who was to have mated with him.

O'Connor sensed this even in that curious half-consciousness. He realised that White Knife would show him no mercy – that he would kill him and take his scalp.

It was at this second, just as he was trying to will his limbs into movement, that he thought of Gentle Fawn. Of course, Gentle Fawn had kept quiet, knowing that White Knife the Indian of her choice, was stalking him around the camp. He felt bitter because after all he had saved Gentle Fawn's life at the risk of his own.

That tomahawk in the hand of the leaping Indian was already thrusting down for a death blow when a ferocious cat-like form struck White Knife in mid-air and sent him reeling. Only it wasn't a cat. It was Gentle Fawn, and she was almost spitting in fury as she scratched and fought with a bewildered White Knife.

Careless struggled on to an elbow. He could hear Gentle Fawn's sobbing words. White Knife must not kill Oak-O-Nur. Oak-O-Nur was a man above men and he had saved her life, Gentle Fawn's. For that Gentle Fawn was Oak-O-Nur's, and while there was breath in her she would not see him harmed.

Amazed, O'Connor saw her strike and batter at White Knife, driving him away by the very ferocity of her attack. And because it was not an Indian's way to make war on women, White Knife retreated unresistingly.

Then Careless staggered to his feet, the blood streaming down beside his face. Dazed and dizzy, he lurched over and picked up his rifle.

White Knife saw the action. He turned and raced off towards the undergrowth. O'Connor threw the gun up to his shoulder and sighted. White Knife's bounding form was an easy target for him. His finger tightened on the trigger. And then it relaxed.

Slowly he lowered his gun. He couldn't shoot down a man in cold blood like that. He had never shot a man in the back before and he wasn't going to start now.

O'Connor turned and saw that Gentle Fawn was looking at him. There had been horror on her face when she saw that rifle raised, but now a flood of relief came over her beautiful bronzed features. Her head slowly drooped and he felt there were tears in her eyes.

Then she came stumbling towards him, and went down on her knees and clasped him round his torn and dusty jeans. Her soft young form was shaking with sobs, the reaction after the murderous events of the past few seconds.

She was moaning: 'You are my master. You are a man above men. Only a great man would have spared his enemy thus. It is not an Indian way.'

O'Connor put his hands on her glossy hair. 'It is not an Indian way,' he agreed. 'But it is a good way. That way you make friends.'

He knew then that if he had shot down White Knife it would have turned Gentle Fawn against him, because he could see that after all Gentle Fawn thought a great deal about the young brave who had been her chosen mate. As it was, in saving White Knife's life it bound Gentle Fawn to him with even stronger ties.

He lifted the girl to her feet, sighing. His arm about those shaking shoulders, he wondered if after all he had been right in sparing White Knife's life.

For White Knife, knowing of this massacre, would assuredly seek out his own people, the mighty Sioux tribe. And that meant – war! For the Sioux would never permit the wiping out of one of their tribes to go unavenged.

'By tomorrow,' O'Connor thought grimly, 'the hills will be alive with Sioux warriors on the scalp trail.'

He brought his thoughts round to immediate matters. He saw where Gentle Fawn had hidden the horse when he had seen the crouching figure of White Knife in the bushes. Now he threw her on to the saddle and stiffly mounted himself. Now he must get back to the railroad camp to give warning of what might be expected.

Wearily they set off over the mountain trail that they had so laboriously followed in the past many hours.

SEVEN

BUTCHER SHOWS HIS CARDS.

Someone spotted the solitary horse and its double burden when they were a mile out on the hot desert.

All along the railroad working men stopped to watch their approach. There was an uncanny silence for a few moments as men leaned on their mighty sledgehammers and held back the tumbling rails from the flat cars. Even the engine drivers stopped shunting.

They saw a man and a girl wearied beyond relief. On a horse scarcely able to walk another mile. The three were caked in dust where it had merged with the sweat on their faces and bodies. For a moment they were not recognised.

And then someone said: 'By gar, that ees O'Connor!'

Instantly the sharp-eyed half-breed's words were

taken up and passed along the line. O'Connor's back.

Joe Butcher got the word in his cabin along the track. He came lurching to the door, tired himself after the long night and day on the trail, yet not showing it because he was an iron man. He came out and shaded his eyes against the morning light.

Then he began to walk slowly along the track towards the advancing riders. As he went he gave little signals and unobtrusively men began to fall in by his side and walk with him. So it was that when O'Connor drew rein and peered through eyelashes that were caked with dust, he saw Joe Butcher and a grim-faced party of brutal-looking workers striding down to meet him.

He got off his horse. When his feet touched ground, he swayed and could hardly stand. Gentle Fawn was watching him, somehow confident that this resourceful giant would find means of protecting them both.

O'Connor stirred his weary limbs and went forward to meet Joe Butcher. They were all walking with their hands on the butts of their guns now. It needed one word, one signal, and lead would instantly be thrown.

O'Connor knew it. Knew that even if he came up with his guns first and triggered them before his enemies, yet still they were too many for him and inevitably he would be mown down by the blasting lead that would come from those many more guns.

Yet no signal came. Perhaps no one wanted to take a chance on stopping O'Connor's lead before he went down. Or perhaps it was they were so confident that they did not want to dispatch their enemy too quickly.

Joe Butcher's voice rang out harshly: 'You've been causing quite a bit of trouble around here, O'Connor!'

O'Connor knew that the provocative voice was intended to get him to make an incautious move.

His own voice came croaking up from a throat as dry as the desert. 'Mebbe,' he agreed mildly.

They faced each other, tense and watchful. On the trucks on the railroad that ran beside them, men looked down on that scene and waited for gun talk.

But the weary Texan was looking at those spectators now, rather than at his adversaries. He was trying to estimate the support he might get from them.

He was arguing to himself that though last night they had wanted to lynch him, yet with a night's sleep to wear off the effect of alcohol and cunning talk, many of these men would be ashamed of their previous conduct. He might even find friends and supporters among them.

So, though he talked to Joe Butcher, arrogant and confident among his tough, unsmiling supporters, his words were really addressed towards those listening ears up on the flat cars.

He said, loudly, roughly, 'You know what you've done by last night's work, Butcher?'

Butcher smiled, a hard, evil smile that was without mirth. 'We evened a few scores with them pesky Injuns,' he snapped. There was a roar of approval from the men standing alongside him.

O'Connor said, clearly so that all could hear. 'You rode out an' massacred an Injun village. I've seen 'em, an' you didn't leave one of 'em alive!'

Butcher tried to defend himself against that extreme accusation. 'There was a fight,' he bluffed. 'We beat them Injuns up, but it was no massacre. You're lyin' to try to get me in bad O'Connor!'

Perhaps it was just at that moment that Joe Butcher realised he might have gone too far, and that if this big Texan opened up with any more truths he, Joe Butcher, mightn't be able to count upon the support his confidence had said he would get from his men.

O'Connor told them all, 'It was a massacre. I reckon you got into that camp afore they knew what was comin'. Ef you don't believe me, ask this gal here. That's why I brought her back. She's got no kinfolk left.'

He rubbed away the caked mud from his forehead. Under cover of the movement he watched the effect of his words upon those listening men. He saw one man drop to the ground and come marching steadily towards him. He recognised the man. This was the man who had been with Riordan's party that had helped him the previous night. The man's eyes were blazing.

'Is that the truth?' the man thundered as he marched up.

'It's the truth,' Careless said. His voice carried conviction. That rough-looking railroader wheeled upon Joe Butcher. 'Man,' he shouted, 'are you mad? Don't you know what's goin' to happen now?'

Joe Butcher was suddenly uneasy, because he could sense an antagonism flaring up among those men. They had followed him only while the liquor was in them. Now they were ashamed at what they had done the previous night.

He snapped, 'I don't care what happens now. All I know is you've got to be tough with these Injuns. When they come a-tomahawkin' right into our very camp, that's the time we should go out an' teach 'em a white man's a white man!'

His supporters roared approval at that, and some of the men had their guns out as if to intimidate the workers up on their flat cars. Hundreds of men were now gathering around that scene in the desert, attracted from all along the line. Not a man was working now.

O'Connor told them what would happen. 'The Sioux nation will be ridin' the war trails afore tomorrow.' His eyes were like cold steel as they looked at the author of their trouble. 'And that's just what you want, Joe Butcher,' he snapped.

That brought all men's eyes upon him. He went on to explain – 'Back of Joe Butcher is a pack of no-good politicians in Washington. They want power, an' they seek to discredit the present Government.

'So they've got Joe Butcher in their pocket, payin' him well to get this Federal-financed railroad well behind schedule. That way they think to discredit their political opponents.'

Dimly only most of those men understood what he was saying. It was mostly above their heads, because they were simple, rough, working men. But what they did understand was sufficient for them.

A man up on a stack of ties howled down, 'Goldarn it, you mean to say Joe Butcher's deliberately brought the Sioux out on another war just to stop this railroad goin' through?'

Joe Butcher tried to shout down the answer that O'Connor gave. 'The man's lyin'! We just went out an' gave them Injuns a lesson! That's all there is to it. O'Connor with his talk about Washington politicians is just tryin' to make more trouble!'

But O'Connor waved him aside. 'Boys, it is as I say. If you don't believe me, just wait a couple of days or so, then you'll see that skyline swarmin' with Sioux warriors. Then you'll know who's right – Joe Butcher or me.'

Many of those men didn't need to wait. What Careless was saying had a ring of truth about it. Besides, in moments of soberness they were not impressed by their loud-mouthed brutal-mannered boss ganger.

Men in sudden fury came flocking down from those flat cars and crowding in nearer, all shouting and waving their tools as weapons.

In a moment it was obvious that though Joe Butcher had many supporters, they were outnumbered. The one thing in their favour at that moment was that mostly they were armed, while the railroad workers supporting O'Connor were without anything but the tools they carried.

Some of the men began to run to where their rifles were stacked. Joe Butcher knew the situation was desperate. He shouted, 'Stay where you are! You take another step towards them guns, an' we'll open up on you!'

His own brace of Colts were in his big hairy paws. His supporters had their guns levelled, too, and at that the threatening circle of workers began to give ground.

The little island of Butcher supporters stood back to back with their guns bristling outwards. O'Connor moved back with the others. When he came alongside his horse he slapped it hard and sent it shambling away, the girl upon its saddle.

If there was going to be any gunplay he wanted Gentle Fawn to be out of reach of any stray bullets.

Joe Butcher caught the movement. His guns swung round and covered O'Connor. 'You step this way, big fellar,' he said sarcastically.

O'Connor looked at him. Then he looked at those guns. Then deliberately he went walking backwards towards that friendly, encircling crowd. His hands were hovering a couple of inches above the butts of his guns.

He called across the intervening space. 'No, sir. I ain't puttin' myself in your murderous hands. An' if you try to put lead into me, I'll live long enough to get a brace of shot into your skin.'

Joe Butcher knew he meant it, too, and that delayed his trigger finger long enough for O'Connor to be swallowed up by his friends. Tom Riordan was there, unexpectedly, and Tom's broad figure deliberately stepped between O'Connor and Butcher's guns.

For just a second no one moved. No one knew

what to do. Tom Riordan settled the matter.

He said, 'I'm goin' to report this back to head-quarters by telegraph, Joe Butcher. I reckon they'll send for you to answer questions for last night's work. You'd better put down your weapons an' wait an' see what comes back by telegraph.'

Joe Butcher's red, heavy face snarled with sudden temper. He was not the kind of man to be crossed. He shouted, 'Like heck I'll put down my guns! Not with him about!' His gun lifted again, trying to find O'Connor in that crowd.

O'Connor saw the man whisper something, an order to his men. They began to shuffle backwards, retreating out of the circle. No one made a move to stop them, because they were formidable with their bristling array of guns.

When the gang were outside the ring of hostile, silent workers, some of the men ran away to get horses. When they came riding back, leading spare mounts for Joe Butcher and the men who had stood their ground, a roar of anger rose from Tom Riordan's supporters.

Riordan shouted, 'You're not ridin' out of trouble like this, Joe Butcher! You've got the Sioux Nation on our tail, an' now you think to ride out of the country an' leave us at it!'

Joe Butcher, swinging into his saddle, grinned. O'Connor knew what was in the man's mind. He was thinking that nothing mattered now, that he had done his work well. With the Sioux on the warpath, the railroad project was at a standstill for months. His friends in Washington would take full advantage of the situation and would amply reward him. He could afford to feel cheerful.

Back of the crowd that grinning face aroused the ire of some stalwart labourer. Something came whizzing through the air. It was a heavy piece of chain, consisting of about four links.

Joe Butcher tried to pull his horse round quickly, but he could not escape the full force of that blow. The swinging chain smashed against his chest and shoulder, and the force of it felled him from his saddle.

Instantly the horse went crazy, lashing out and kicking up a great dust.

Butcher's supporters came racing round to try to help their chief, and one of them took a swift shot at the man who had hurled the chain, but missed him.

But that was the signal for a running battle to start among those trucks and dumps of railroad equipment and crude tents and huts that littered this patch of desert.

Everyone went streaking off to find weapons, while the Butcher mob dragged their groaning, pain-racked chief behind the shelter of a stack of sleepers.

O'Connor and a few of the others with guns opened up to save their scattering fellows from being shot down by Joe Butcher's trigger-happy gunmen. Then everyone dived for cover.

Behind that hut the mob got a horse to their chief and hoisted him into the saddle, and then unexpectedly the whole mounted bunch came streaking out from cover and heading straight for where O'Connor and his few armed supporters were crouching behind the flat cars.

Riordan shouted, 'They're after you, Careless! Keep down!'

Then brave old Tom knelt and tried to fight the horsemen off. Other railroad workers were just running back now with their guns, but they were too far away to intervene.

Joe Butcher leapt his horse right in among the defenders, his face black with fury. He was cursing O'Connor as he came driving in, his spurs biting so deeply into his horse's sides that it screamed with pain.

Behind Joe Butcher came the other gunmen. They came in with weapons flaming amid a mighty cloud of dust that had been kicked up by their horses' hoofs.

In one second, it seemed, they were in among the defenders, shooting and trying to get to where Careless was fighting desperately with his back to a wagon wheel.

For a few moments it was impossible to tell friend from foe. Lead smacked into the wood alongside O'Connor's head, and bullets spanged against the steel wheel spokes and ricocheted off.

He fought back desperately until his guns were empty. While he fought he was thinking, 'Joe Butcher wants me out of the way. With me out of the way he might bluff Washington, but he knows a Federal agent's word carries weight!'

They were out to silence him, and that meant killing him.

They would do it, too. There were too many of

Butcher Joe's men milling around, and too few of Riordan's supporters.

In fact, the one thing that saved O'Connor just then was the fact that there were too many of Joe Butcher's supporters, all trying to get at him and getting in each other's way momentarily. But that was something that would not last indefinitely. Any second now one of them would get a clear aim on him and that would be the end of Careless O'Connor, Federal agent.

With empty guns in his hands O'Connor leapt to his feet, the fatigue of the past few days forgotten with the imminence of death. He saw a horse stumbling out of the ruck towards him, and he drew back his hand to hurl his Colt at the rider.

Then the horse wheeled and he realised that it was his own, finding strength from somewhere to race through to its master.

And clinging to its neck was the black-haired, brown-eyed Indian maiden, Gentle Fawn.

She was calling to him in Kittewa. He didn't understand her words, but he knew what to do. As his gallant beast swung away he grabbed a stirrup leather and then swung himself on to the bare back behind his saddle. Twisting, he looked back at his enemies. They were trying to pull out and race after him, and their guns were blasting lead in his direction. But the speed of his escape saved him. No one found a target.

There was little strength left in his horse now, though, and Joe Butcher's mob would run him down within seconds, he knew. But ahead of him, running stumbling over the uneven desert towards him, came the railroad workers with rifles in their hands, plucked from the stacks that were always close to where they worked.

O'Connor shouted. The men flung themselves down and pulled off the safety catches and opened fire. Joe Butcher's men seemed to fade away at that ferocious fusillade.

O'Connor let his horse run to a standstill behind that line of defenders. They were safe now, he knew.

Wearily he dismounted and reached up and helped the girl out of that high saddle. He stood there, his hands gripping her shoulders, and smiled down at her fondly.

'Much more of this, Gentle Fawn, an' I sure will be changin' my mind about gittin' myself a squaw!'

Gentle Fawn understood. She smiled, a gallant smile, and then turned away. Because she knew O'Connor never would and it made her heart break to think of it.

They waited for Riordan to come doubling back from their line of wagons. Riordan shouted, 'Some of them varmints have set fire to the store sheds south of the camp!'

At that all the men went streaming off to prevent a spread of the blaze. O'Connor and the girl walked wearily into the town.

He took her to the crude saloon where he bunked, and found her a room next to his own. He locked her in for safety and then went and stretched himself on his own bunk. He was sure there would be no danger now, with the entire town out looking for Joe Butcher and his mob.

He had no intention of sleeping, for all his need of it. There was important work to do, but he had to rest, and lying there proved fatal to his plans. He fell asleep immediately.

It was many hours later when he was awakened by a thump on the door. The sleep had worked wonders with him. Now he felt fit to meet anyone – even an enemy.

With reloaded guns he stepped to the door and called, 'Who's there?'

It was Riordan and some of his friends. 'We thought it was time we had a parley with you,' Tom told him, walking into the room and sitting on the plank bed. He looked worried.

'Injuns?' Careless was rolling a cigarette.

'Nope.' Tom shook his head. 'But I reckon they won't be long afore they come. There's smoke signals been seen west of the track. That's got a bad sign.'

O'Connor nodded. Those smoke signals would be summoning the chiefs of the many Sioux tribes to war council.

'They won't be long,' he agreed. Then he asked quietly, shrewdly, 'What do you want of me?'

Tom's face was almost lugubrious with worry. 'You're a Federal agent, Careless. You're kind of – official. We ain't got no sheriff nor anyone to lead us an' advise us. An' now Joe Butcher's pulled out, we ain't even got a boss. We're kinda lookin' to you to help out.'

Careless said gently, 'Help out? Sure? But you tell me all about it afore I get to givin' any advice. There's somethin' mighty unpleasant bin happening

111

while I was asleep, I'm figgerin'.'

Tom sighed and his eyes travelled hopelessly to the faces of those other defence committee that had been set up. 'Mighty unpleasant,' he agreed, and told Careless of Joe Butcher's latest audacity.

The wires were down. Joe Butcher had torn them down to prevent any news of his infamy from being telegraphed to Washington. But it also prevented them from sending out a call for troops to help them if the Sioux appeared.

'Wuss than that,' Tom said, 'he's clean lifted the track right where it goes into the canyon. We're stuck here in the desert. We can't relay them rails 'cause Joe Butcher an' his men are settin' right on top of the bluff, ready to open fire the moment we come in range. I guess that critter's gonna keep us all penned this side of the mountains until the Sioux swoop down an' complete the destruction for him.'

'We're stuck on the desert? Can't get away anyhow?'

'You tell me how men on foot c'n cross this hyar desert an' live? We've got a few hosses, but they can't take a thousand men. We've sent three riders skirtin' round the canyon to give warnin' in Tulverville, but you know how long it'll take 'em to get there? Three days – ef they don't meet Injuns.'

'Three days?' Careless looked out of the window. Well within three days the mighty Sioux would be raging upon them. If they were to be saved they had to work out their own salvation.

His face grew grim, thinking of big, brutal Joe Butcher, who didn't give a hang how much people were hurt so long as his own pocket was well lined. Butcher, he sensed, was going to sit astride that break in the track and hold them there at the mercy of the approaching Sioux.

That would be disaster, just as the unscrupulous politicians wanted it. And Joe Butcher would collect his ill-gotten reward when the recital of destruction was thoroughly completed ...'

Tom said hopefully, 'Wal, you got any ideas?'

Careless grinned. 'Some.'

'Such as?'

'I'm goin' to get me the biggest jug o' cawffee in the camp.'

'An' then?'

'I'm gonna get me the biggest meal I've had in days,' he smiled, ambling casually towards that door as if he had all the time in the world.

Tom got exasperated. 'Goldarn it,' he exclaimed, 'this ain't no time for foolin'.'

In the doorway Careless turned and said, 'I ain't foolin', brother. You know what they say about condemned men? They always eat a hearty breakfast.'

He looked out through the glassless window. The sun was almost down in the west.

'I'll have my breakfast now, a bit early,' he grinned, and they heard him go into the passage and tap softly upon the door of the next room. They followed out into the passage.

O'Connor opened the door and Gentle Fawn was standing within, timid now, and afraid because she was within a white man's lodge.

O'Connor put his arm around her shoulders reassuringly. He was getting mighty fond of her, he thought. And that thought was in the minds of quite a few of those men watching them there. Tom voiced the general thought: 'Looks like you're goin' to mate with an Injun the way you're goin' on, Careless.'

His voice was not altogether approving. But Careless shook his head, his eyes grim.

'Nope, pardner, I ain't got such thoughts in my mind. A Federal agent don't hardly get the chance to make himself a home, I reckon.'

They were moving out into the street, to where a chow-house had been erected. Tom was still curious. 'What's gonna happen to the gal?'

So then O'Connor told them of the crazy scheme that was in his mind. 'Mebbe she's gonna be a passport for our safety,' he said. 'When we've eaten, we're both gonna ride to meet them Sioux warriors. Ef Gentle Fawn's the gal I think she is she'll tell them Sioux that that massacre was the work of a plottin' connivin' no-good white man, an' it's no good tryin to take it out of other white men where in this camp. Mebbe I can talk the Sioux back into their territory with promise of compensation.'

But all those men there looked at him aghast. Tom exploded: 'Careless, you're sure plumb right off your head! Them Sioux'll take off your scalp as soon as they set eyes on you. Careless, you haven't a chance!'

EIGHT

'CARELESS' ' MISSION!

It was dawn in the high lands. Two riders relaxed as the warming rays of the morning sun dissipated the cold night mists that had chilled them to the bone.

As they came to the top of a pine-clad hill, where the trees had been bent into fantastic shapes by the bleak and unceasing winter winds, they paused. Halting their horses, they looked carefully around them.

Below, the country was rugged and wooded, still green in these heights though the land they had left below was almost desert in this midsummer.

Careless was uneasy. This was not a mission that he cared for. He knew it was the most desperate he had ever entered upon, and he knew there was little chance of success for him.

Kinship was strong among the Indians. To kill a blood brother, however remotely connected, demanded, according to Indian code of honour, vengeance to the full.

Yet because of the plight of those railroad workers, stranded at the end of the line they had constructed, Careless was willing to take a big risk and try to turn the Sioux warriors back from the war trails.

He had met the Sioux chiefs in times past and knew that they respected him as a man of honour and justice. He was gambling on meeting those chiefs and being able to get them to call off their men before a war started.

Careless could truthfully tell them that whatever minor successes might greet their first raids, in the end the white man's guns would win any war against the Sioux people. After Custer's recent battle against them, he knew his words would weigh with these chiefs.

But would he be able to meet the chiefs in war council? More likely, he thought grimly, he would be speared out of hand by the first group of Indians he ran into before he had time to ask for their chiefs.

Westward from the point where they stood their horses, he saw many spires of smoke climbing into the brightening sky, and he knew this to be an Indian camp.

It must have been a big camp, too, he thought looking at the many columns of smoke. Because of the intervening hills he had no means of estimating the size of this Indian force, but he was willing to bet that here was a good part of the mighty Sioux tribe.

Shaking the reins of his faithful horse, O'Connor turned downhill in the direction of the Sioux camp. His eyes were alert as he went, because with such a big force so close at hand he knew there would be patrols of Sioux warriors keeping watch in these hills.

Gentle Fawn suddenly spurred up to his side. Indian-like she had not spoken to him since the start of the journey. She had followed docilely, riding a few yards to his rear as befitted an Indian woman with a warrior.

Now those camp fires moved her to conduct which would have been considered unmaidenly among her people. Careless felt her hand grip his arm, and he turned. She was pointing towards the smoke spires in the distance, and there was a question in her eyes.

Careless understood. He nodded. 'Sure,' he said, 'I know them to be Injun fires.'

'They will kill you,' Gentle Fawn said swiftly.

'Mebbe.' Careless had an uncomfortable feeling the girl was right. 'I've got to go through, anyway,' he said doggedly.

Those hundreds of men marooned along that railway line had to be saved if at all possible. Even if it meant risking his life, he had to try to help them.

O'Connor's horse shied. The big man felt that the beast was uneasy over something, and he noticed how the ears pricked forward and the eyes rolled. He reined. A horse was better than a dog for giving warning any day.

Gentle Fawn had ridden up to his side again, sensing the danger that was in the air. Together they sat their mounts, and with sharp eyes looked into the brush around them.

After a while O'Connor said: 'I cain't see anythin', but that don't mean to say they stopped their manoeuvrings.' He smacked his horse affectionately on the neck. 'This old nag ain't often wrong when it comes to smellin' Injuns.'

Gentle Fawn nodded.' I feel – danger,' she said softly.

Then they saw danger. A man rode out from the trees below them. He was a brave in the war-paint of a Sioux warrior.

He was a bold man, deliberately risking a bullet. He sat his mount below and looked up at them insolently, his paint-daubed face frightening to look at.

A moment later another horseman came walking his mount through the cover twenty yards to the right of the first warrior. He, too, reined on the single head rope that was the Sioux fashion.

O'Connor knew what to expect now. Another warrior appeared, this time twenty yards to the left of that first warrior. And then other warriors came out from the bush, all at twenty yard intervals from each other and forming a giant crescent around the edge of the basin below them.

All told there must have been thirty braves in that party.

O'Connor hadn't made a move until they stopped their manoeuvrings. He had been sitting his horse calmly, leaning forward on his saddle. He took out a pipe that was only used in times of great danger. It was more comforting to him then than a cigarette. While he lit up his keen eyes never left those silent menacing Indians below him.

Gentle Fawn whispered: 'Turn and ride. I will try to stop them. My lord and master must save his life.'

Big O'Connor, the sun glinting on his brown,

battered features, grinned, and said: 'I ain't runnin' now. An' I ain't your lord an' master.' He nodded towards the Indians. 'That's where you belong. You'd better git yourself across to 'em right now afore any fun starts. An' make yourself useful – tell 'em I want to see their chiefs. Tell 'em I have big talk to make with 'em.'

Gentle Fawn shook her head. 'If my lord and master rides into their hands he will surely not live to see the sun set. When a Sioux warrior puts on his war-paint he does not take it off until he has killed.'

Her finger suddenly stretched forward, pointing. 'See how they are holding their spears!' she exclaimed. 'They want to kill, and will kill!' And she would not ride forward as Careless wanted her to do.

O'Connor said doggedly: 'Okay! I'm goin' forward, even so.'

Boldly he rode a hundred yards down that grassy hillside, and perhaps the audacity of his move stayed the charge that had been imminent.

Even so, O'Connor was no fool, and did not place himself within range of those stabbing spears before he held parley with them.

When he was fifty yards away, with Gentle Fawn faithfully riding by his side, he halted again. His repeater rifle was across his saddle bow. If these braves wouldn't accede to his request to be taken to the chieftains, he wouldn't hesitate to use his gun. Careless felt that his life was as precious as any Indian's.

Lifting his left hand, palm facing towards the Indians, he spoke in his best Dakota. He called that

119

he was a friend, that he wished no harm to the Sioux but would help them. He demanded to be taken to certain chieftains, and he gave their names.

The leader of the party spurred his horse forward at that. Instantly O'Connor was crouching in his saddle, that deadly repeater cradled under his arm. It brought the paint-daubed Indian to a sudden halt. The Sioux knew all too well the deadliness of those repeating rifles.

O'Connor called: 'You don't need to come right up to me. I ain't gonna walk into your hands, brother. Just lead the way to your camp an' I'll follow.'

That was as far as he was prepared to entrust himself into Indian hands.

But that Indian wasn't to be satisfied so easily. He grunted and gesticulated, demanding the surrender of that deadly weapon.

O'Connor stuck the pipe back in his mouth and shook his head. His eyes were grimly humorous. 'Not on your life!' he said.

For a few moments there was stillness. Then the Indians conferred among each other.

Gentle Fawn whispered to big O'Connor: 'They will agree to lead you to the Sioux camp because you will not surrender your gun. But they mean treachery.' She was a Kittewa, and knew how treacherous an Indian could be.

'They will wait for a favourable moment and then they will hurl their spears into your back,' she prophesied. 'You will never see your friends, the Sioux chiefs. These warriors are scalp hunters and will not let you fall to any other hunting party.'

O'Connor nodded. She was probably right. But still he was determined to go through with his plan.

So when the Indians ahead nodded and indicated that they would lead the way and he and Gentle Fawn should follow, he lifted a hand in acknowledgement.

Inwardly he felt some satisfaction at what had happened. He felt that he had so far won. Perhaps in spite of what Gentle Fawn said, these Indians would take him to the camp of their leaders and then he felt certain that his counsel would prevail.

Warriors might want war, but the powerful men of the tribe, the leaders, he knew would be against it. If he could tell them the truth of what had happened – if he could tell them that the miscreants would be punished and the Sioux compensated for the massacre of their brethren he was fairly confident they would take their men back into the Sioux hunting grounds.

The important thing was to meet those chieftains face to face. He gripped his rifle. Whatever Gentle Fawn said, he wasn't going to let any Indian get around him to throw a spear into his back.

They set off slowly, walking their mounts over the rough ground. And all the while O'Connor watched for signs of treachery. His eyes looked to see the Indian who might slip away into the brush and prepare an ambush for him as he rode past.

But the braves rode steadily onwards through the crowding vegetation in single file, and not for one moment did he see the slightest suspicious movement.

Gradually big Careless O'Connor relaxed in his smooth saddle. He even smiled at Gentle Fawn.

'Reckon you sure misjudged them,' he said. 'I didn't think the Sioux were nearly so bad as you made out.'

He checked himself quickly. He had nearly said, '—like your Kittewa people.' But though it was true, though the Kittewa tribe was notorious for its double dealing, it was hardly the thing to say to this lovely representative of that massacred people. Anyway, Careless was sure that Gentle Fawn was straight enough.

He was suddenly so confident, exulting as he rode under that hot, rising sun. In his bones he felt that he was going to win out, after all. And it was a fine achievement for a man to contemplate – that single-handed he might prevent a formidable Indian war.

'Jes' let me get talkin' to them Sioux chiefs an' they'll call off their people,' he told himself determinedly.

It was at a moment when he was certain that Fate was being kind to him and he was going to ride on under safe escort to meet the Sioux leaders, that disaster hit him. There was no other way of describing it.

Suddenly he saw movement among the Indians ahead that had every appearance of discomfiture. He saw them pull off the game trail they were following, dragging their ponies aside quickly like men who wanted to be out of the way.

Out of the way of what? O'Connor instantly wanted to know. His grey eyes peered under the shadow of his hat brim to where the Sioux warriors were uneasily flanking the pathway.

A solitary figure was stumbling towards him. An Indian. An old man without any feathered head dress but who wore a cord around his black greasy locks. He was naked save for a breech cloth, though around his middle was a string on which were threaded the bones of some small animal.

He was small, sinewy and looked the colour of the earth over which he trudged.

O'Connor watched as he advanced towards him, and he wondered why those Sioux warriors had pulled away from him in such distaste – or was it fear?

For O'Connor was sure this man was not a Dakota, and why should these Indians fear one from another tribe?

Careless let his eyes flicker to where Gentle Fawn had reined in her pony beside his own. She was looking towards the advancing old man, and her eyes were widening with terror.

O'Connor's head jerked round. His eyes looked suspiciously forward to where the Sioux warriors were gathering back on the trail, looking back after that solitary old Indian. Yet plainly they had no hostile intentions towards O'Connor. Of that he was certain.

Their thoughts at that moment were evidently all occupied by the aged Indian who was now within twenty yards of O'Connor.

The big Texan leaned forward in his saddle. He could understand Indians being afraid of some old man with a reputation for powerful medicine

making, but it cut no ice with him. He had no superstitious fears and consequently he watched the
approach of the line-faced Indian without any appre-
hension.

He could see that face clearly now. It was incredi-
bly old, ravaged into deep lines by a long life under
a pitiless sun on these mid-Western plains. It was the
kind of face that looked almost as if the owner had
become mummified, and it wasn't pleasant to look
upon. O'Connor was certain he had never seen this
man before.

Then the man's eyes seemed to open. At any rate,
when he was only ten yards from O'Connor's tired
horse the Indian lifted his eyes and met those of the
big Texan.

Then Careless wasn't so sure that he had never
met this Indian before.

Again his eyes switched towards Gentle Fawn. He
couldn't understand it. Gentle Fawn was shrinking
away in her saddle, her eyes looking upon that old
man with a loathing O'Connor had never seen on a
human face before.

It rang a bell. Some instinctive danger made
O'Connor turn quickly to keep his eye on that old
man. And the thing that was puzzling him was that
though he had never seen that face before, yet in
some way, looking into those fierce little black eyes
that seemed to glare up at him, he had a feeling that
at some time they had met. It was contradictory, and
he couldn't make it out.

But one thing he did know. This man hated him.

It bewildered O'Connor. Again he turned his head

to look at Gentle Fawn. He turned it because that old Indian did not appear to be carrying arms. At any rate there was no lance or bow in his hand or toma-hawk or knife showing in his belt. There was nothing to fear from some cranky old man if he was unarmed.

Gentle Fawn was sitting there, her face curiously white under that lovely honey-coloured tan of hers. And her mouth was open and seemed to be moving as if silently saying some words. He caught the flash of her white even teeth, and then saw her eyes stare at him and there was horror and dread in them.

As he turned his head again to watch that old man he had an impression out of the corner of his eye that Gentle Fawn was just lifting a trembling finger to point towards the old Indian.

Then O'Connor saw the old man almost under his horse's nose. He saw him make the swiftest of move-ments with his hands into his breech clout.

The next thing he knew, that old man, fanatical hatred blazing in those eyes, was lunging towards him, pointing a Service Colt into his face.

At which moment Gentle Fawn screamed in the agony of one too late to help the man she loved. O'Connor, going backwards in his saddle, heard her scream change to a moan and through it all came words, and they were, 'It is that man! That man who made bad medicine for my tribe!'

It was his old friend, the Kittewa medicine man with his ceremonial mask off!

NINE

THE BOLD PLAN
FAILS.

O'Connor remembered thinking, 'Goldarn it, of course I couldn't recognise the maverick!'

But even as he was thinking that, his lightning thoughts were creating a pathway to safety for him.

Already he was jerking backwards in the saddle before the threat of that lunging pistol. And the medicine man, sure that the white man's fire stick was more powerful than Oak-O-'Nur's medicine, seemed loath to pull the trigger and end the life of a man whom he hated.

All the same the fingers started to tighten on the trigger as O'Connor reeled away in an instinctive act of self-preservation. O'Connor's foot was out of its stirrup in a flash and kicking hard under the armpit of that triumphant medicine man.

The swiftness of the action upset the medicine

man's aim. The gun arm jerked up and the pistol blasted off but aiming towards the bright blue sky.

In the same moment O'Connor stabbed out again with his foot and caught that medicine man and sent him reeling a dozen yards away into the dust.

O'Connor still hadn't gone for his guns. He did not dare reach for them in case it brought the Sioux warriors back against him. He had played so carefully to win their support that he could not lightly throw away his gains just because of the hatred of one old discredited medicine man.

So he kneed his horse around, making an elusive target of himself as the medicine man came clawing on to his knees in the dust, that Colt gripped in his skinny old hand.

O'Connor was shouting, trying to get those Indians in the distance to understand that this was no fight of his choosing. But while his voice was ringing out Gentle Fawn came spurring her horse between him and the medicine man. More, as she came level with that old man she threw herself from her saddle at him.

That was the bravest thing O'Connor had ever seen. It took courage beyond that of ordinary people to attack a man reputed to be a powerful maker of medicine – especially of bad medicine.

But sure in her primitive mind that this man who had saved her life so often was in danger, Gentle Fawn was prepared to give her own life if it gave O'Connor a chance to save his own.

The old medicine man screamed his hatred as the girl fell against him and gripped that gun arm and tried to tear away that heavy Colt. He was an old man, but with a ferocity that was something like madness he yet had the strength on her.

He flung her away.

She seemed to fall on her knees, and in the same moment come up on to her feet again, running round immediately to attack that old man.

O'Connor saw the old Indian's gun jerk up and point at the girl. He knew there would be no mercy in that evil man's heart, knew that in a second poor Gentle Fawn would have given her life to save his.

That was too much for Careless O'Connor's patience. His heels kicked viciously into the ribs of his horse. It reared in protest and anger, and that gave O'Connor extra height so that he saw over the head of poor Gentle Fawn. For just a second the girl's slim figure did not cover that of the murderous old medicine man.

In that second O'Connor's gun leapt out of its holster and jerked forward into flaming hatred. And the bullet beat the old man's trigger finger.

Dazed, Gentle Fawn saw the old man topple backward and then roll over – dead.

O'Connor was shouting. He wheeled and grabbed the reins of Gentle Fawn's horse. He was watching those Dakotas along the pathway ahead of him, and he knew what was going to happen.

As he dragged Gentle Fawn frantically into her saddle, he saw that troop of Indians come wheeling round in a flurry of hoofs, and he knew they were going to begin a death charge on him.

He had failed! These Dakotas had seen a white

man kill a red brother – more especially, a powerful medicine man – right before their eyes. That was something that had to be avenged on the spot. Besides which, sight of blood sent those young braves scalp-crazy immediately. Nothing now would stop them from seeking Careless' scalp.

A wild bloodcurdling scream rose from those savage Dakota warriors at sight of their prey beginning to turn and run from them. The sound was enough to frighten all but the stoutest-hearted.

O'Connor, cursing the ill luck that had led him to cross the path of that medicine man just at that moment, heard Gentle Fawn sobbing beside him.

Perhaps some of this was on his account, but he guessed she was in fear of her own life, too.

For Gentle Fawn had attacked a medicine man in defence of a white man. The Dakotas would not spare her after witnessing such an act.

As he put his horse to the hill again, that hill down which they had just ridden, O'Connor shouted: 'You don't need to worry, gal. I've got some good friends with me.'

He patted his Sharp's repeater and the butt of one of his Colts.

When they were clear of the brushwood that clothed the lower part of the steep bank, O'Connor shouted to the girl to bring her horse down to a walk. The slope was severe and already their mounts were gasping.

The Indians whooped with delight when they saw their victims proceeding at little more than a walking pace. With savage abandon they flogged their wild-eyed, saliva-flecked ponies into a mad gallop at that steep slope. It was just what O'Connor wanted.

Some arrows came zipping up towards them. The aim was good, too, O'Connor noticed, but they were saved by the movement of those staggering, climbing Indian ponies.

O'Connor fired back, sitting round in his saddle. His repeater never missed a man.

Before the deadly fire those Indians lost heart and pulled precipitately away.

But it was only for a few seconds. Their blood was up and they were in superior force. They pulled away fifty yards or so towards the vegetation, and then they recovered their nerve and came storming up the hill again after the pair.

But it had gained Careless a few more precious yards towards the safety of that top. And they were walking their horses, resting them as much as possible, while the Indians were forcing theirs beyond endurance.

O'Connor kept firing steadily now, and again he drove off the first of the warriors.

Again he gained precious seconds and made those Indians lose ground on the hillside, ground which they had to get back with much thrashing of over-worked ponies.

They got to the top of that hill. O'Connor again emptied his gun into his pursuers, and that held them back for more precious seconds.

Now O'Connor shouted. 'Git a-goin' gal!' And he clapped his heels into his mount and sent it at a steady gallop down the long slope beyond. Gentle

130

Fawn kept pace by his side.

The first of the Indians reached the top of that hill. Their horses were exhausted by the ferocious effort that had been demanded to climb that slope at speed. Now the Indians' ponies hadn't the breath left in them to raise a gallop after the white man and red girl.

O'Connor's bold tactics had given him an advantage – an advantage he had no intention of forfeiting now.

They gained the better part of a half-mile lead before the Indians' ponies were rested sufficiently for them to begin the gallop in pursuit.

O'Connor never lost that lead. Resisting the temptation to force the pace unduly in the beginning, he beat off any bold attackers by calmly halting his horse and carefully picking off his enemies as if he were at a turkey shoot. Then he would turn and gallop after Gentle Fawn.

Two hours later and the pursuit was over. These Indians could not match tactics with this bold white man, neither had they weapons to equal his Sharps seven-shot repeater.

By nightfall O'Connor was again riding across the desert towards where men stood idly around the end of the track. When they saw the trail-dusty pair returning, the town came gathering to see them. O'Connor's quick eyes noticed the defence preparations about the town. And then thought how poor they were and wondered why greater effort had not been made to throw barricades between the huts. He saw, though, that all the railroad men were now

131

carrying arms wherever they went.

Then he saw a man in a blue uniform.

He stared at this man. It was the uniform of a trooper of the United States cavalry.

Tom Riordan came pushing through the throng that was shouting questions at the pair. Tom's face was beaming with gladness. He reached up and shook O'Connor warmly by the hand.

'I sure am glad to see you, Careless. I didn't reckon you would come out of that Sioux territory with your pretty hair still above your ears.'

Then the men everywhere grew silent, and O'Connor knew what they were waiting for. They were waiting for him to tell them what had happened in his parley with the Sioux chiefs.

'Folk,' he called out, 'I never met them chiefs.'

He saw a man close to him. A man with tobacco-stained teeth and several days of beard on his chin. The man's face had turned to a sneer at O'Connor's words.

O'Connor said quietly: 'I did my best. I nearly made it, too. I'd met up with a passel of Injuns on the warpath, and they were taking me back to meet their chiefs.'

Then he went on to tell of the ill-luck that had brought that hating medicine man down the path at that moment.

Tom called up: 'I thought that galoot was leading Joe Butcher's gang against his own people?'

'He did that,' O'Connor nodded. 'I don't know what he was doin' away from Joe Butcher's mob. Mebbe when he'd served his purpose, instead of giving him the reward promised they kicked him out.'

Maybe all he got for turning traitor on his own people was one stolen Colt gun which had led to his own death. That theory seemed to fit the situation and Careless guessed it would be right. No wonder that medicine man had looked so crazy and had been so keen for vengeance upon a white man.

The crowd was still waiting. O'Connor said: 'I reckon no one'll get near them Injuns to talk with 'em for a few days. I figger we've got to hold 'em back somehow. We've got to fight for our lives.'

There was the trooper in the crowd. A big, overfed man, though the cavalry were supposed to run to spare men. He was looking contemptuously over the heads at O'Connor, sitting there beside the Indian girl.

That trooper called: 'The major says you're scarin' yourself to death. He says the Dakota won't take no more war trails after the thrashin' they got a coupla years ago.'

O'Connor had no time for fools. He snapped: 'Then what's the meanin' of them smoke signals that went up yesterday? And how come the Sioux have a big camp back in the hills – a mighty big camp, judgin' by their many fires – an' they've got war-painted riders out guardin' the trails.'

The big trooper just said: 'The major says—'

But those railroad workers, who had little love for the army, turned on him angrily and shouted him down.

All the same, when O'Connor was sitting on his

plank bed listening to Riordan and some of his friends, the boss ganger said: 'This major's one of those darned bigheads that won't listen to sense. An' the trouble is he's officially in charge of this project. Ef there's trouble that bonehead will be tellin' us what to do.'

His voice was disgusted. O'Connor wanted to know who the major was and all about him.

Only that day, Riordan told him, they had been surprised by the sight of a major and half-a-dozen cavalry riding in from the northern desert. They hadn't realised that any army unit was within five hundred miles of the end of the track.

When the major arrived he told them that he had ridden over from where the Cavalry Regiment was bivouacked over the Furness Mountains.

When O'Connor heard that he seemed to stiffen, sitting there, but he did not interrupt while Riordan told the story of the major's arrival.

'We told him about the Kittewa trouble and that we feared the Sioux would come seekin' vengeance.' Riordan slapped a mighty fist into an equally mighty hand in exasperation. 'You wouldn't believe the way that fellar just looked coldly at us, an' said: 'You are imagining things. You can take my word for it that the Sioux will not take the war trails again after the last defeat our army gave them".'

Riordan said: 'You can't argue agen the army. They think they know everythin'. So we told 'em about the line bein' bust back east an' how Joe Butcher was coverin' it so that we couldn't get out of this desert.'

134

O'Connor grinned. 'What did the major think to that?'

Riordan snorted. 'He didn't believe us.'

'So?'

'So we sent him down the line on a loco to see. He's not come back yet. We reckon mebbe he ran into trouble with Joe Butcher, an' if he did I think I'll feel mighty glad to know it.'

O'Connor said: 'He's comin' back now.' Through the window he could see the solitary saddle-tank chugging in from the east. Leaving Gentle Fawn in the adjoining room, Careless and the other men walked down to the track to meet the loco. The major was on the foot plate. He wasn't looking so happy.

They had to help him down. He had been shot and he was indignant about it. The shot had been in the seat of his pants, and he had lost a little flesh and it was mighty painful for him and he couldn't sit down.

He kept saying indignantly: 'I would never believe it! They opened fire on us! They wouldn't even listen when I shouted out that I wanted to talk to them.'

Riordan said bluntly: 'Joe Butcher's shot his bolt and he knows it. All he wants now is to bust this project and then he can collect a mighty lot of money and go an' live in some other country like Mexico a rich man for the rest of his life. He jes' looks to the Sioux to finish off what he's started.'

They helped the unbelieving major away, finding a bed where he could lie face down. He was still insisting that the Sioux would never take the war trail.

135

'Military intelligence would have known about it if so,' he kept saying.

Big Careless O'Connor grunted. 'Makes you sick to listen to the durned fool, don't it?' And then he said: 'Look Tom, how about gettin' a rider over the Furness Mountains to bring in the cavalry – without lettin' that fool major know what we're up to?'

'I'd do it like a shot. I'd go myself. But how far could a rider get in those mountains durin' night time? He'd pitch over a crag an' break his durned neck. I reckon we'll send one when it's light tomorrow.'

'Yeah?' One of the committee was sarcastic. 'What good will that do us? By the time he reaches the cavalry we'll be just a hair fringe on a Sioux warrior's lodge. Nope, you've got to think of a quicker way of gettin' warnin' through than that.'

Careless looked to the blue hills to the north and sighed. A horse was the fastest means … Careless' news about the Sioux war party had caused the railroad workers to go frantically at the work of barricading the perimeter of their camp. Careless watched with a feeling of depression in his heart. Barricades weren't going to hold back their ferocious, determined enemy. He said so to Tom. 'This won't stop the Sioux. Goldarn it, Tom, you should see them red devils when they hit the war trail. I reckon there's five thousand o' the varmints back of them hills. Ef they're not here tonight they'll be on these plains by first light tomorrow.

'Have you ever seen the Sioux fight? They're the finest, darndest fighters you've ever set eyes on.

They'll be stormin' through these defences as if they don't exist by noon tomorrow.'

Tom shrugged helplessly in turn. 'All right, what do you suggest, big fellar? Not put any barricades up?'

Careless toed the dirt-grey desert soil. 'Nope. I reckon you're better behind barricades. But I always reckon when things are bad to look for the unexpected to win battles for you.'

'Meanin'?'

'Meanin',' growled big Careless, 'I'm gonna do some thinkin' tonight. I reckon there's a way out for us an' I'm bettin' it's starin' us right in the face. By tomorrow mornin' I want to have the solution to this darned problem!'

Tom called after the rangy figure: 'You'd better think it up quick, fellar, else we'll all lose our scalps tomorrow!' He was grinning to himself as he watched that big figure recede along the huts. He had a mighty respect for Careless O'Connor's ingenuity.

There was no alarm during the night, not that any was expected after nightfall, for the Sioux, like most other Indians, do not like night fighting.

But the town was awake before dawn, every man-jack of them, standing behind those barricades and looking with tensed, grim faces towards those hills to the south and west of them. It was from that direction they expected the Sioux attack.

O'Connor was out with them, shivering a little in the thin air of the morning. Gentle Fawn was at his side. Some of the men were hostile towards her, not forgiving any Indian. Careless thought it safer for her

to be with him than back among the huts even
though locked in a room. Some of these desperate
men might get up to tricks with her while he was out
of earshot.

Gentle Fawn was timid and did not like to meet
the eyes of those rough railroad workers, standing
with their rifles behind the piled sleepers that mostly
constituted the barricades. She never moved more
than a few inches away from O'Connor's side.

Tom saw the big Texan silhouetted against the
morning sky that was grey before the first yellow rays
of sunlight climbed above the eastern horizon. He
lounged across and spoke to Careless.

'You got any hunches in this night?'

Careless was looking across the barricade. Tom saw
that big, flat battered face of the fighting Texan and
knew his answer.

'Nope? Then I reckon we ain't got much chance of
seein' another night,' he said, and walked across to a
defence post. Tom Riordan was going to give of his
best while ever he had a bullet left in his gun and
breath in his body.

Careless knew that that could go for most of these
men here, anyway. They would fight, but they would
be hopelessly outnumbered and against the finest
fighters in the world. They wouldn't last long even
behind the protection of their barricades.

So his eyes probed into the gathering light, seeking for an enemy and hoping not to find him. As the
sun lifted and cast its first rays across the desert, the
morning mists almost instantly dissolved and they
were able to look into the distance where those hills

138

began to mount off the plain.

A high-pitched croaking cry arose from some old-timer's throat. The old man's shaking finger was pointing. 'Injuns! There they are!'

Every eye slewed in the direction of that gnarled, pointing finger. They saw a low knoll about a quarter of a mile away, rising off the plain. Among the trees were silent, unmoving figures. Men on horses. Men with feathered plumes that told of war bonnets.

Indians! The mighty Sioux Nation was on the warpath!

Then someone growled and cursed and pointed in another direction. Heads slewed round. As the darkness retreated before that rising sun it revealed more Indians silently watching from the summit of another hill due south of them.

Then a shout brought their eyes round to more Indians west of them.

There was a gasp from those railroad men. There must have been thousands of silent, waiting Indians stretched in an enormous line to the south and west of them. Truly the whole nation was out.

It brought dismay to even the stoutest-hearted there. Men stared and couldn't believe their eyes. And then trembling hands lifted guns and took sight across the barricade tops and waited for the charge that would annihilate them.

Yet as the sun climbed fully over the horizon, those Indians did not move. They were like statues. And because they did not move, did not start their terrifying war charge, curiously it brought a greater terror upon the defenders. Panic gripped a few of them

and they were seen to stumble away from the barricades, not knowing where they were going and yet
wanting to flee.

Big Careless jumped across and grabbed one of
them and hurled him back towards the barricade. He
was shouting: 'That's why they're doin' it! Don't lose
your heads, darn you! Them Indians want to get the
rabbits among you boltin' out into the desert, then
they'll cut you down like … rabbits!'

His words stayed the beginnings of a panic that
could have become a stampede. Tom Riordan
looked at the fighting Texan and thought, 'We're
lucky to have that Injun fighter among us.'

And then the major limped out to take charge of
the fighting. His face was pale but very determined.
He was also complaining.

'Why didn't someone come and tell me the
Indians were here?' his querulous voice brayed.

One of the railroad workers' committee spat a
brown stain on to the dust and then answered cyni-
cally, 'Last night you reckoned the Sioux wouldn't
attack us. We figgered you mightn't believe us if we
said they was knockin' on the door.'

Something like a guffaw rose from the listening
men, and it made that proud major stiffen. Careless
saw the sharp dark look come into those curiously
faded blue eyes and he thought, 'This fellar can stir
up a whole lot of trouble if he's riled.'

And then, looking at that major, he had his brain
wave. His fingers suddenly snapped excitedly and he
turned and looked towards where those Sioux
warriors were still standing their ponies on the low

hills on the desert's edge, trying to strike terror into the defenders' hearts.

The major was calling, 'I'm going to take charge of the defences. You will obey my orders as if you were soldiers. In fact, from this moment you are impressed into the service of the United States Federal Forces.'

It made men blink. But they were still blinking when that major was rudely shoved on one side by the mighty Texan, Careless O'Connor. Careless was in a hurry and had no time for fools.

Men were looking down at him from their positions on top of the huts and on fire steps made against the high barricades. Everywhere Careless saw grim-eyed men watching him.

He shouted suddenly and passionately, 'We ain't got a chance, fellars, tryin' to defend this town. We'll not get any relief here afore we're wiped out. But there's a regiment of soldiers who could hold back them Injuns while we got that track repaired and pulled out into safer country in the canyon.'

The major was bleating something and trying to shove his way back to O'Connor, but Tom Riordan blocked his way. No one had time for the army officer. They were much more ready to pay heed to the advice of Careless O'Connor.

O'Connor shouted again, 'I'm tellin' you, I know how we can play for time until relief comes to us. It's not by stickin' behind these barricades an' bein' shot down one by one.

'I tell you, the way to lick these Indians is to set fire to this town right now!'

'Set fire?' Instantly there was a murmur of astonishment from all his audience. Then the major came marching back, exclaiming, 'Are you mad?'

O'Connor got impatient. He pushed the major aside again, without any semblance of courtesy. 'This ain't madness,' he exploded. 'Goldarn it, don't you see it's the best thing we can do. This town'll make a mighty blaze. It'll send a smoke signal clear across them mountains and warn the cavalry that there's something wrong along the railroad.'

He didn't need to go on. At once they understood the drift of his argument. They could picture the enormous column of black smoke that could rise from this desert if they poured out those barrels of oil on to the huts and set them off in a gigantic blaze.

'That sure would bring the cavalry in,' some of the men agreed, looking at each other. And then a fireman shouted suspiciously, 'Okay, but what defence would we have then against them varmints? How could we hold them back?'

O'Connor told him. The inspiration had come in a flash.

'There's your garrison!' he said, pointing.

The Texan's hand was outstretched towards the track, with its several engines and many types of freight cars.

'Git aboard them wagons. Git them wheels a-rollin'. That train's as good a defence post as this town. A movin' target's harder to hit than a sittin' one!'

In that early morning sunlight those hundreds of railroad workers could only stand and stare at that big Texan, wondering, hardly daring to hope, and not believing yet.

Someone voiced the general doubt.

'But where do we go? Them wheels might roll, but they wont' roll far.'

Now it was this man's turn to point, and his hand stretched eastwards towards the canyon that bit through the hills towards the rising sun. Those hills in which lurked the saboteurs.

'The track's bust six or eight miles that-a-way, an' it don't go any place westward from this point. What do we do when we get to the break in the track – fly?'

Careless shook his head. 'Nope. I reckon we just reverse an' come back.'

Men stood up at that, their voices incredulous, a clamouring, arguing chorus.

'Goldarn it, shuttle up and down along eight miles o' track?'

'Fightin' Injuns all the time?'

And then they looked at each other. There was something in O'Connor's madness all the same. It was true, a moving target was harder to hit than a stationary one.

A mob of men came round Careless at that, all arguing. Gentle Fawn was terrified and he could feel her clinging to his belt and shrinking into him from behind. But they weren't thinking of an Indian girl then. There was a possible chance in this bold planning of O'Connor's, but they weren't quite ready to accept it yet.

'I reckon we won't do that more'n a few times,' some bristly-bearded track-layer opined. 'Them varmints is cunnin'. They'll start to tear up the track after a time.'

'Sure, after a time,' agreed Careless. 'But that's what we've got to play for. Time. Time for the cavalry to see that signal and start to come ridin' down from the north. I figger it's a ten-hour journey for them, an' it means we've got to hold off them Sioux devils until nightfall. I figger usin' that train might save most of our lives.'

Tom Riordan took a chance. He looked round at those men there and said, 'I don't want to persuade you. You've got to make up your minds same as I'm doin', but I reckon Careless has got a right good idea there. I vote we do as Careless says.'

That major started to bleat opposition. It wasn't military tactics, he was saying. But nobody took any notice of that major in his pretty West Point uniform. These were practical men whose lives were at stake and they weren't going to commit them to any old-fashioned military theory.

Slowly hands were raised. After a time almost every hand there was lifted to signify approval for O'Connor's plan.

Only at that moment did they realise they had been neglectful of the most important thing. No one, in the excitement of those minutes, had been watching the distant Sioux.

Now the mad charge had begun. That desert before them was one solid bank of Indians and ponies, charging in headlong gallop towards the undefended barricades.

TEN

A RUNNING BATTLE!

A voice screamed, 'Too late! They're comin' now!'

A cloud of dust went up as men twisted on their heels and went plunging frantically back to their positions on the barricades.

'Fight 'em off,' roared O'Connor's voice, above the startled oaths and cries of the defenders. 'Drive them away if it's only for a few minutes, then we can fire the town an' git aboard that train.'

Those were their tactics now. But it looked as if there would be no turning back that tide of raging Indian might that was streaming behind fluttering war pennants towards them.

A couple of hundred yards from the defence posts those Sioux warriors let out their frightening war cry. The dust was spurned up from the flying hoofs of those wild-eyed ponies. It was an awesome sight.

Up on the barricades men flung themselves down and drew bead and began to fire. White smoke drifted over the ramparts, and the acrid bite of gunpowder dug into the nostrils of those sweating, harassed defenders.

O'Connor was up on top of a log hut that had been a store shed for the telegraph construction company. When he turned crouching behind a mass of tangled telegraph poles that had been tipped on to the roof of the stout shed, he saw Gentle Fawn by his side. He started to shout angrily at her, to tell her to go away but then he realised he was wasting his breath.

Indian women very often went with their menfolk into battle, especially young women newly betrothed to their warrior mates.

Gentle Fawn still considered herself in that light, he realised, and now she held out her hands to receive his rifle when it was empty.

O'Connor knelt and began to fire rapidly at the screaming, charging horde. The earth seemed to shake beneath the thunder of those tens of thousands of flashing hoofs. The screaming of ponies and the dying cries of stricken Indians filled the air. Arrows came singing viciously in among the defenders, and they were so close that lances were hurled and stuck into the woodwork – and sometimes into the hearts of the cursing white men whose rifles were now empty.

O'Connor tossed his rifle back into the girl's hands to be reloaded. He felt her fumbling in his belt for cartridges, while he blazed off with his twin Colts.

Those Indians were so close now that he could look upon their hideous, war-painted faces. They were near enough to see him and to mill around on their ponies, momentarily defeated by the wall of barricade. Then hot-headed, impulsive braves leapt on to the bare backs of their horses, riding them round parallel to the huts, and flinging themselves

146

on to the ramparts, engaging the defenders in hand-to-hand struggle.

It was almost all over for the defenders with that very first charge.

In fact for seconds not a man there but thought this was the end for the railroad garrison.

Yet in some way the tide was turned – miraculously the attackers were thrown off the ramparts and the small arms of the white men took deadly toll of those close-packed screaming warriors, all pressing to get within the barricades.

Fighting with fury born of desperation, the white men drove the Indians away those precious few yards from the barricades, and then the whole Indian horde wheeled and went fleeing out across the desert towards the protection of those little hills.

The defenders wiped the sweat away from their brows with their forearms and reloaded and took breath again after the exertions of those awful minutes.

Someone grunted hoarsely, 'They'll be back. They don't let up. You always beat back the first charge, but they come and come again until they've worn you down.'

When they looked they realised they had suffered terribly in that first charge. Men lay against the barricades, transfixed by spears and arrows, and a few of them mutilated by tomahawks.

O'Connor shouted to the men to bring out the wounded and get them into the closed freight cars. Already the drivers were getting steam up and men were coupling the engines and trucks together.

Frantically working under Riordan's direction, men

were rolling out barrels of tar and the thick lubricating oil used on the car axles. Cans of grease were split open and hurled on to the roofs of the huts.

In the distance the Sioux warriors were lining up again. Any moment now and that second deadly charge would begin.

Lamp oil was thrown over blankets and bedding, and every hut there was made as inflammable as possible. They were still working on it when a lookout shouted, 'Here they come!'

That thunder again. That scene of barbaric ferocity as those thousands of braves came screaming across the desert, a great rolling grey cloud of dust billowing behind them.

O'Connor shouted, 'Away from them barricades! Fire the town! Then git aboard that train!'

Everywhere men were running with torches. They touched off those huts and anything inflammable within reach. In that dry, hot atmosphere flames leapt to incredible heights within seconds. In an amazingly short space of time those men running towards the railroad track were ringed round with roaring flames that singed the hair off their faces, so tremendous was the conflagration.

It startled the Indians. One moment they were charging a series of barricades, the next they were racing towards a fiercesome circle of enormous flames. It caused them to wheel, and to ride in among each other in the utmost confusion. For minutes on end those Sioux warriors rode around the town, their ponies nimbly leaping the shining tracks that stretched out east and west of it.

But within that encircling ring, the heat was too great for the men to linger. The last man was dragged aboard the freight cars, the drivers signalled to each other and released the brakes. Steam burst into cylinders and moved pistons and the giant train began to move eastwards.

At that the Indians began to leap their ponies through the falling flaming barriers and ride right into the centre of the town. Up on the first engine, clinging to the handle on the footplate, O'Connor saw those terrifying Indian forms bursting through the flaming barrier and streaking towards them.

'Faster, faster!' he roared to the drivers, who opened the control valves to their fullest extent. The long train of cars leapt forward with a great snatching of couplings. Inside the freight cars, firing through the open doors, men shot down the first screaming bunch of Indians. But the others were coming into the town now, and still others were racing across the desert almost flat on their wild ponies' backs, their faces lost in the flying mane of those gallant, hard-pressed little horses.

It became, in fact, a race along those metals. The Indians reached the lines just as the train, gathering speed, burst out of the flaming town and went plunging towards that canyon east of them.

There was a savage running fight alongside the track. Indians raced their ponies as close to the freight cars as possible, discharging their bows and hurling their spears and trying to crash their clubs in among the defenders. A fusillade rang all along that line of jolting, swaying cars. Indians toppled from their ponies, which ran wide into the desert. But though many went down, always there were hundreds more to take their place.

But the finest pony still could not keep up with several engines cramming full steam into their cylinders. At a pace incredible considering the state of the new-laid track, that train rocketed   eastwards. For just a few moments the ponies held their own, and then they began to drop behind, and at that a mighty cheer arose from those men.

There came a time, in fact, when the Indians were a quarter of a mile behind those rolling cars, and were pulling up in fact, as if abandoning the chase.

Then they came to where the track was up and that train had to stop, and they were within sight of those avenging Indians.

Wiping the sweat and dust from his eyes, Careless leaned out from the cab of that engine and stared at the canyon ahead. The canyon floor was like a smooth ribbon of rock, completely cleared and levelled by the construction engineers.

On either side of the track the walls reared abruptly, almost overhanging at this point, they were so precipitate. And right on top, among the trees and vegetation, Careless saw movements.

Joe Butcher's mob still covered the canyon with their rifles, determined to hold back the railroad men and thus create as much damage to the railroad project as possible.

Along the line of freight cars men leaned out, and shook their fists at Joe Butcher and cursed him luridly. If those men could have laid hands on the man at that moment they would have torn him limb from limb.

Musing, Careless looked ahead to the break in the track. For a couple of hundred yards into the canyon itself the rails and sleepers had been completely removed. They had even been hidden from sight, probably to prevent any attempt at a swift repair under cover of darkness.

Beyond the break the lines gleamed brightly in the morning sunlight, a pathway to safety but one they could not reach because of the break in the track.

Careless descended to the sun-baked earth. Gentle Fawn was at his side immediately. Then Careless flung her back against the engine as a bullet zipped into the sandy soil just by his feet. He climbed back into the cab, pushing Gentle Fawn before him.

'Them varmints don't intend to let us set foot on this soil,' said Tom Riordan grimly.

Then they all turned to look back westwards along the track. In the distance they could see the mighty column of smoke that came from the burning camp. It must have been all of two thousand feet high, a broad, densely black pillar of smoke that must have been seen for fifty miles around.

Careless thought, 'Them cavalry will be seein' that. Ef they don't come to investigate, their commandin' officer sure will lose his rank!'

They would come, they all knew that. But would they come quick enough? It was a race against time, with their lives at stake. The estimates were eight to ten hours for the cavalry to cross that northern range. But could they hold out against those Indians as long as that?

They looked to where the Indians were massed along the track. Time passed. Then the Indians must have decided to come along and investigate the reason why that train was stopped within their sight.

They had rested their horses by now and came surging along at their usual fast gallop. Careless waited until they were a couple of hundred yards from the two engines that had been pushing at the rear of the train. Next time they moved they would be pullers, and the engine Careless was on would be the pusher.

Careless leaned out and waved and there was a responsive wave from the cab of the furthermost engine. Instantly a jolt ran down the line of trucks as the two engines took the strain. Slowly the train gathered momentum. When the Indians came racing level with it they were already proceeding at a good pace.

The men on those freight cars looked out on a sea of milling, baffled redskins who had never had to fight a mobile fortress before. They charged the cars, doing a lot of damage with their arrows before wheeling and careering out of range.

Again the train pulled through and gained such speed that it left behind its Sioux pursuers. Onward they rolled, until finally they were nearing that blazing construction camp. Then the brakes were applied and gradually, with a lot of bumping, the whole train came to a halt.

Men jumped down to stretch their legs and rest and attend to the wounded. Fires were quickly lit and coffee made and food served out.

All the time sharp-eyed men were watching back along the track, where a couple of miles away the

Sioux forces were gathering in baffled rage to look after their elusive target.

A couple of hours passed. Precious hours. By now surely the cavalry must be well on their journey, men thought and hoped.

Then the lookout called to Riordan and Careless. 'Them varmints is up to somethin'!'

Careless and Tom climbed to the top of a freight car and looked forward along the track. They saw a group of Indians, tiny dots in that distance, walking towards the track. A long time passed, while the Indians stood on the track as if conferring and planning.

Then they went away and immediately Careless said, 'You know what that means? Them Injuns opine to cut the track again and stop us from being able to roll away from 'em.'

He turned, cupped his hands around his mouth and bellowed down the line, 'All aboard! Here's another trip through hostile territory!'

Cursing but eager, the men clambered back into their uncomfortable transports.

Careless waited up on his car until he saw a large force of Indians on foot run across towards the track and begin to work on it. Then he gave his signal for the train to start another crashing run eastwards.

They roared up to where the Indians were working on the track, sending them reeling back in confusion. Looking down the railroad men could see that already ties had been loosened and sleepers withdrawn. They had crossed just in time! They went on that remaining short distance to the end of the track by the canyon and then slowly and reluctantly came to a clanking halt.

When they looked back they saw the Indians had resumed work on the track. The Sioux were an intelligent people and were proceeding logically to the task of exterminating their enemies.

Another hour or so passed. The sun was already falling westwards. It was uncomfortable in that train, and mostly men were silent, lying about or watching westwards. Only occasionally did they shout threats up at Joe Butcher and his waiting mob. Sometimes Joe Butcher answered it with a shot that was derisive in itself.

After a time it became evident that the Sioux warriors were massing again, preparatory to riding down the track towards them.

Tom Riordan said, 'What do we do now, Careless? Up steam and crash through 'em again?'

Careless said, 'This time they won't bother to attack the train if we do. I reckon they're cunning. I figger they've got the hang of these tactics of ours and they opine to ride round us an' cut the track between us an' the canyon. That won't leave us much line to manoeuvre on.'

'So?'

The situation seemed hopeless. It didn't seem possible that they could hold out for another three or four hours.

O'Connor's eyes were looking back along that hard, smooth rock floor that went between the high canyon walls. He was thinking that he didn't want to get away from this canyon, didn't want to be trapped farther out, there in the open desert. He was beginning to get an idea about that canyon—

He gripped Tom by the arm. 'Tom, I've got a hunch. Ef that hunch don't work, we'll be in a worse position than ever. I don't know whether we dare risk it.'

Tom said, 'If there's a chance of cheatin' these varmints until sundown, I reckon we ought to take it, Careless. They've got the measure of us now, an' a couple of hours an' we'll be a sittin' target for them.'

Careless took a decision. He knew all those lives depended on him, but he was a bold man and was prepared to gamble even with his comrades' lives. He said, 'Okay, Tom. Then listen to me.'

Riordan listened and then he gasped at the audacity of O'Connor's scheme. He said, 'Sure, we've got dynamite. But will—'

O'Connor said, 'But nothin'. I'm gonna do it. Now you watch out for my signal.'

He ran down to one of the trucks and foraged about for some dynamite. O'Connor found Gentle Fawn with him. He said, 'You get aboard this train an' stay there. You ain't comin' with me on this journey.'

A shout of alarm spread down the line. The Indians were racing towards them across the desert. Careless had to work fast!

He got what he wanted including a small pick, and then he ran back towards the engine, keeping close to it for cover. When he came to the break in the track he paused a moment and then went flat out across the intervening space towards the shelter of the canyon wall. He made it, too. Probably his action was so sudden that it surprised Butcher's mob. Nevertheless bullets spanned hatefully down at him long before he reached shelter. Fortunately he was moving elusively, zig-zagging, and the lead missed him.

It missed Gentle Fawn, too. When Careless reached an overhang at the base of the cliff, Gentle Fawn was standing there beside him, her hands meekly clasped together, her eyes smiling adoringly at him.

Careless opened his mouth, then he shut it. There was no arguing with this girl. But he had work to do.

He began to pick holes into the rocky base under that overhang. That done, carefully he inserted the sticks of dynamite and began to set fuses – long fuses.

All the time the swelling roar of that Indian advance was in his ears. He could even distinguish their war cry above the sound of those pounding hoofs. And on that train he heard desperate men shouting, 'Get them wheels rollin' darn you! Can't you see they're a-comin'!'

The men didn't know what Careless was up to. They were frantic now, as the Indians, suddenly very bold, came storming in towards the stationary wagon train.

Careless, sweating as he worked with frantic haste to fix the explosive, finally leapt to his feet and waved his hands above his head. That was the signal.

Instantly the train surged forward. It trundled on towards the break in the track. Men shouted with alarm as the tracks jolted together all along the line. The Indians were already up to the rearmost engine, and were sweeping in towards the slowly-moving freight cars.

The men in the cars were having the fight of their lives to hold back those Indians, and all the time the train was slowly gathering speed.

Fascinated, O'Connor watched the leading engine run right off the track. For one second he thought it was going to topple over. If so every man's life there was forfeit to the hunch that had come to him.

Yet in some miraculous way that engine stayed upright on a rock as hard almost as the steel rails themselves.

The trucks began to jolt off the line, but again all stood upright. And all the time that engine was plough-ing forward along the rock into the canyon itself.

O'Connor took off his hat and cheered, he was so delighted. It was the first time in his life he had ever seen a train running on ground instead of rail! And yet it worked.

Gradually that entire train load of freight cars and engines was pulled off the track and went trundling along the rocky canyon bottom.

Careless struck a match and lit a fuse.

It was just at that moment that an Indian suddenly came from nowhere and snatched Gentle Fawn away from him.

There were men in those freight cars who saw it happen and they gasped, for it was unbelievable.

It seemed as if this mounted, naked brave came springing out of the earth. It was so unexpected. Even so Careless had his revolver out and pointing and should have been able to shoot the brave off the back of his pony before he came racing up. But whether Careless shot and missed they never knew, because there was too much noise all around them to distinguish a single shot.

All they knew was that that Indian swooped in,

picked the Indian maiden up on the run, then went wheeling away towards the main Sioux force. And even then, marksman as he was, Careless should have been able to shoot down that Indian.

Gentle Fawn was fighting to be released, and the last they saw her hands were outstretched towards big Careless O'Connor under that overhang, as if beseeching him to come and save her.

It was all over in a matter of seconds. Then the last engine ploughed into the canyon, while from all the freight cars men were tumbling out and racing back to guard the entrance against the Sioux.

For a moment they held their own. The mighty Sioux force was held back beyond the entrance to the canyon. Then Careless came tearing away from the rock face shouting, 'Run for your lives!'

The Indians started a mad charge from out in the desert, seeing the railroad men fleeing up the canyon. They were coming in towards the narrow canyon entrance when all at once the face of the cliff seemed to blow out across the gap. Rocks were hurled high into the air and splinters came flying out to meet the Indians, who promptly wheeled away in terror.

Up the track the railroad men watched in awe. They saw the bottom of the cliff blow completely out. And then the landslide started. A huge crack developed up the face of the cliff, and at once the whole mass began to slide down into the canyon mouth.

Someone shouted, 'Look! Joe Butcher!'

Right on top of the bluff, riding down into the depths of the canyon as if on an ice flow, Joe Butcher and his men came crashing down with the landslide. For a moment those saboteurs were to be seen standing on ground that was flying through the air. Then they disappeared from view amid the crashing rocks and the rising cloud of dust.

That was the end of Joe Butcher and his mob undoubtedly. No one could survive such a disaster.

Tom Riordan wiped his head. 'I reckon he deserved what he got,' he pronounced, and no one wasted any sympathy on men who had been prepared to forfeit the lives of their comrades for the sake of money in their pockets.

They looked at the barrier that had now fallen clear across the canyon mouth, sealing them off from the desert and the Indians beyond.

Tom said, 'You've done it, Careless! I hand it to you. Them Indians can't get over that barrier within hours.'

Cheering men came up to shake Careless by the hand. They knew they had won now. Before any further hostile act could be taken by the Indians, the cavalry would be down to reinforce them. Meanwhile, they could try to get their rolling stock on the lines and then roll eastwards.

Careless was thinking of his report and how he would nail those offending politicians in Washington for this. Things had worked out fine. Even Tom Riordan wasn't worried about this fall of rock across the track and of the interruption to the schedule.

'We'll pick that up within a fortnight,' he vowed. 'My men are fightin' mad now. They'll work like beavers. We'll have the railroad constructed on time,' he declared.

And then he looked at Careless. He said, 'I reckon it was tough about that gal o' yourn.'

Careless said, 'My gal?' There was humour in his tone.

'Sure.' Tom was looking at him quizzically. 'Careless, if I hadn't seen that with my own eyes I wouldn't have believed it. You're not the kind of man to miss an Injun at such close range. Yet you let a blamed Injun pull one over on you. That's the only time in my life I've ever seen you licked.'

'Sure I was licked,' said Careless, meekly.

And then he walked away, thinking about that defeat – if defeat it was. And he was thinking that Gentle Fawn was much better off with her people, especially better off with that warrior who had risked his life for love of her – that war-painted brave who had snatched Gentle Fawn away from him.

White Knife!

Sure, he thought, she'll be better off with him.

There was no room in Careless' fighting life for a girl. And then he sighed, waiting for the sun to go down and the cavalry to come in.

She was a lovely girl, and she could have been his so easily.

He took out his pipe. It was his friend on the lonely trails and a solace to him. He lit it. It was a solace now. Two puffs and he was the old Careless O'Connor. And he was thinking, 'Where next?'

Already he was itching to be off on another hazardous mission.